Spire Publishing

www.spirepublishing.com

Strange Fruit

Avenda Burnell Walsh

Spire Publishing
www.spirepublishing.com

Spire Publishing, June 2008

This edition first published in Canada and Great Britain 2008
by Spire Publishing.
Spire Publishing is a trademark of Adlibbed Ltd.

A cataloguing record for this book is available from the Library and Archives Canada. Visit
www.collectionscanada.ca/amicus/index-e.html

Designed in Toronto, Canada by Adlibbed Ltd.
Set in Baskerville and Baskerville Italics.
Printed and bound in the USA or the UK
by Lightning Source Ltd.

ISBN (10): 1-897312-75-X
ISBN (13): 978-1-897312-75-9

Spire Publishing
www.spirepublishing.com

Chapter 1

THE DEEP SOUTH

Old Loula pulled an upturned pail nearer the bench and eased her feet onto it. She leant back and watched the chickens. 'My name is Loula,' she told him eventually. 'There was a time they used to call me Young Loula, though that was a powerful long time ago. But now they calls me Old Loula. Try as I might I can't never recall the moment between the two. It seem like it happen overnight and there was my youth gone. One minute I was Young Loula, swanking long straight legs under my cotton skirts for all to see, titties moving and keeping the fellas' eyes agog, then one day I see they was calling me Old Loula. And I takes a look and I am old too, legs paining me if I walks too fast and paps all dry and thin, still swinging away but like as not in two different directions. It come as a surprise to me, I can tell you.

'Anyhow, this story is not about me. Probably on account of my life is just about finished now.'

Old Loula looked over at the smart man who had arrived that morning in a dust free car. He nodded to her, yes, go on, he was interested to sit awhile and hear what she had to say. In fact he had driven a long way to hear this. Driven back over many years.

The listener had gone straight to the small collection of houses rather than find the hotel first, not at all convinced he would stay. It depended on what he might find. The houses were little more than shacks, which for some reason surprised him. He had left his laptop in the car, sheltering it under a blanket to keep it from cooking in the hot sun, and had poked around for a while, expecting some memory to click into place, but everything remained strange to him. Eventually an old woman had walked up to the seat near the faucet and now it seemed he had got her talking. She was shriveled and sour looking, her hair gray and spiky. God knows how old she was, he'd decided, but she must be old enough to remember.

'You asked about a young child used to live here,' Old Loula, was saying. 'That child grown to a woman now, in body at any rate but where her mind is half the time we don't know. We think we have all the pieces of the story just about tied up … we is myself and the two other women who mostly sit at the spigot of a afternoon, that is Sissie Jane and Libby … but who can tell? This poor child didn't have no happy life so far, and the future don't look so good for her, but maybe the same can be said of most. Things probably started to go wrong when she was about eight year old.

'The child's name is Hester and she was always crying about something.'

* * *

'That child screaming again?' said Libby.

I was just walking up the path to the spigot but Libby and Sissie Jane had filled their pails already. They was in no hurry and fetching water was social time. Years back Solomon set the bench at the spot to confirm the function and this was where we met, us three women … and we was old then … Libby hobbling on her crooked bones and her bad feet, her skin stretched tight and shiny over her great hams. Sissie Jane, the midwife, nearly six feet two, lean and knowing most things a body would be called upon to know, and me, Old Loula. What they said of me I don't care to tell. My body was lean even then, but not mean like some said, and I never was as cross as it sounded. Words just took a turn between my thinking and my mouth and come out wrong often as not. Together we three met every day and fixed the world back together from our seat here at the water spigot.

'She always screaming,' said Sissie Jane, 'since the day I pulled her screaming from her poor mammy's body as if it were Jonah I was extricating from the whale. Eight years she been screaming, that's how long.'

I can see Libby now, shifting her weight from one round buttock to the other as she sat listening to Sissie Jane, a woman whose most formidable weapon was her religion. There was no disputing it was her religion, like she owned it or something. She called on god to support her in every argument and it seemed from his words like most times he did, though he was liable to contradict hisself from day to day depending on Sissie Jane's argument of the moment. Libby was like to say as much to me, but was regularly too polite to mention it direct. Sissie was the midwife and medic that all folk used on account of her not needing to be paid. Not with money anyhow, 'though she never had been averse to a pie or other such thank you. No black folk called in the doctor less you was dying and even then it was wisest to hold fire and keep the money by for the funeral. That was how it was. What Sissie Jane couldn't fix with a remedy wasn't like to be cured by no doctor anyhow. That was what Libby said. It was what most folk reckoned, to tell the truth.

I hobbled up to the others, my feet near as bad that day as Libby's, though my problem was short-term from where my chipped enamel pail, full of water, had blacked my toenail two days before. Now Libby had awful feet. She was famous for the size of her bunions. They come from wearing her one pride and joy in all her life, them red high heel shoes, a size too small when she first got them, and she grow'd a couple sizes up from that before they wore clear through.

Now Libby was a daydreamer and a impractical soul, but she was well traveled. If it hadn't been for her bunions she may have gone further still. And she had the red shoes to thank for her feet. At least my old pail done me better service before paining me.

Libby, like most folks around here, still wanted to learn the full story concerning the pail, thinking there was something mighty precious I had exchanged for it in my youth. I'd had that old pail since I was young and pretty, in a time when new enamel pails were not easy come by. Many speculated what valuable thing it was I traded for my prize but I never did tell nobody the whole story. Young Loula I was then. Looking at me now, wrinkled and gray-dry, some would find it difficult to believe that I might once have had charm enough. I knowed the rumors, and for as many as claimed me the village flirt over that old enamel pail there was a equal number as dismissed the idea as unbelievable. Cross Old Loula, they said? Never thinking I could hold my tongue long enough to be wooed by a man. How easy they forget.

That is another story. Let us get back to that day at the spigot.

As I recall Libby shuffled her bulk further up the seat to give me room, so I set down my empty pail. I would get my water after we set the world to rights.

'Hester always screaming 'bout something,' I said, 'it being on account of she kilt her poor mammy, I suppose.'

'No way did she kill her mother,' Libby defended, standing up and shuffling her weight from one bunioned foot to the other. 'You always saying that.'

'Well her mother spirit sure pass someplace that day, like the Lord hisself I reckon.' Tall Sissie Jane was doing the reckoning; I just set there and listened from that point on.

'Seem to me it pass right back into the child as she was birthing,' Sissie insisted. Sissie Jane should have known if anyone did. She was the only reason Hester was born alive because she pulled the unborn child from the body of her dead friend. Sissie Jane knew the child was alive inside the dead body. She knew before she arrived in that small cabin. She knew before she set off running on the journey to attend her. That's why she ran.

Solomon woke her in the night to tend his wife, crashing against the bolted door until it splintered the wooden cross bar and burst open, with Sissie Jane still struggling between dream and life as he crossed the few paces to her cot and pulled her awake and from the bed, throwing his own coat round her.

'It's awful bad.' That's all he would say, and all he could picture.

It's awful bad. The blood puddled on the mattress, coming too quick to be soaked up, little Joey awake with the screams and huddled frightened under the table, his eyes grown too big in his head.

They flew out of Sissie's cabin and she ran so hard Solomon kept falling behind. But she never waited, just kept on running. It was up to him to catch his breath and try to catch her back up if he could. Poor man, spent from doing all he could do … fetching the midwife. Sissie, six feet two and most of it legs. All her lean body just made for running to cabins in the dead of night to snatch back lives.

'You know it's too late,' she told him, just once, as they ran, throwing the words back to him in the wind.

He nodded to himself, yes. But what else could he do than run? Run there and run back. There was nothing else to be done.

Sissie saw the spilt blood long before they got there. And something else too. She felt the child's pulse pounding in her own head. Sometimes she

10

felt things like that. There was life there to be had, if she got to the cabin in time, she knew, but she had to get there soon. Sissie Jane's feet were thumping, her blood pounding, the baby's pulse pumping in her too. It would be herself that burst next.

The room was as she'd seen it in her head, pictured either from Solomon's thoughts or directly across the half mile space from her own cabin ... her friend spent, the blood pooled, the boy little Joey staring up from under the table. The woman was too old to go having babies, but Sissie Jane had her knife ready, against her calico nightdress and under Solomon's jacket.

Sissie thought she was too late, because her head had stopped aching now and the pulse was gone. Or was there just the barest movement of another's blood through her skull that made her set to her task just as urgently as if she was sure to win.

It's not good for a child to see his mother butchered. Joey witnessed life, almost life, pulled from death, stolen from death. Sissie Jane guessed it was air the new child needed as much as blood so with the chord knotted good and tight, she set about blowing her own breath on the tiny face, gentle at first, as if to waken it. The rightness of the action made her bolder, made her wipe away the blood and fat to cover the mouth with her own, blowing in, then pulling away. Pumping fragile lungs as she would a balloon, then letting them down. It was all she could do. There was nothing further to be done. At last the air was gulped in without her, gulped in and cried out.

Of the three of them, only Sissie Jane thought it for the best. Solomon, not a young man, had lost a wife and gained another helpless mouth to fend for, and Joey would never feel right about a sibling that cost him his mother.

It was only then that Solomon himself cried out. Sissie Jane thought it might have been the first time he spoke in all that while.

'Don't let them burn her,' he said.

'Pardon?'

'She said it over and over. Don't let them burn her. First she asks if it's a girl,' said Solomon, 'but the child ain't born yet and it seems she don't know. Tell her to take my hand into the water, that's what she said, rather the water than the flames.'

Solomon was in a pitiful state. His wife dead on the bed, covered in a soaked red sheet. The new one meowing.

'And something else,' he told Sissie Jane. 'She said, we choose the water.'

Sissie made Solomon sit down but it never shut him up. We choose the water. It was him saying it now. A man with nothing left except his woman's last, nonsense words about taking the child's hand and leading her into the water. Better the water than the flames. Water, the friend of all women. Water, the soother. Water, some trump card against the flames. I recall that one in particular, said Old Loula the narrator to her listener. Water the dowser of fire. About women holding hands and walking to be saved rather than be tried and doomed by men. It may be Sissie Jane didn't tell us all that right off, admitted Old Loula, shifting her feet on the upturned pail. It might be we pieced them parts together as we went along, but that's the long and the short of it. It was something poor Solomon would never reason. The only water for miles around is a small crick. We live a thousand miles from the sea but it seem she was talking of the sea. By the time we found out its true meaning, Solomon had left this life to join his woman. Perhaps he can ask her direct to explain it all.

That night, the night Hester was born, Sissie wiped Solomon's face with a clean patch of her nightdress and handed him the baby. Hester was the name his wife had chose for a girl but she hadn't left instructions for a boy's name. Then Solomon and Sissie both looked for little Joey. Two children he had to raise now. It seem Sissie had decided she best change out the redness of the calico nightdress before comforting the boy but then, with Joey knowing the dress she wore for his mother's, he wouldn't be cuddled against it anyhow.

Eight years later and the child Hester was running to where us three women was sat at the spigot. She was running away from the house as fast as her legs would take her and we was blind then not to know what was starting up with old Solomon, her pa. Although like as not Sissie Jane knew. She was astute in that kind of thing.

'You looking peeked Young Hester,' said Libby, the fat one. Not that it mattered to young Hester just then, who couldn't see which skirt she was grabbing at through the tears. With no mammy of her own it didn't much matter to the child if it was Sissie Jane's strong arms wrapped round her or Libby as pulled her onto the squashed space left between her short arms and her heavy bosom.

On this occasion it was Libby as held her. Hester sniffed back her crying and smelt up a smothering of Libby's breasts. Breasts and milk must of held a wonder for a child starved of her mother from before she was born and fed goat milk suckled from a rag, even I could see that for all I never had children of my own. Libby was the one with babies and grandbabies all over the place. There was no real smell of milk from Libby of course, what with her youngest Zac turning fifteen that year and not even living in the community once he was able to make his own way. The smell was just woman, a luxury for Hester who lived a lifetime away from it, what with the grease of her brother Joe's coveralls, and her father Solomon's shirt sweat, and the stained sheets as she had to wash.

'Tears again Young Hester?' I asked her.

Sissie looked at me scornful like, as if I had spoke harsh to the girl but that wasn't what I meant it to sound like. Sissie said I was out of patience most times and in that she may be correct.

'You and Mary Ellen not been playing at the crick, have you, round by Sally's place?' asked Libby making a point of sounding kindly, which I can only assume was for my own benefit. I didn't mean to be harsh sounding but that girl seemed to be crying a lot them days.

Hester shook her head, no. Going to the crick was something they must never do for they had been told, she and all the children, to keep away from Sally's place for she was a evil woman. We had to say that, back in them days, on account of we was morally superior god fearing folk and it seemed like Sally wasn't afraid of no god. Either that or she was ignorant of his good book, that was what Sissie Jane said and she knew the book from cover to cover for all she couldn't read a word. Seeing as we couldn't read neither, except for Libby who had learnt once but didn't keep no books on hand to practice with, we had to believe Sissie Jane was right in this boast of knowing all the Bible words, but some days I wondered if she wasn't pressing truth a bit farther than it really went.

Anyhow, none of the children knew what evil it was Sally performed in her cabin out there by the crick but some of them older boys used to watch her from the trees and seen the trail of grown men paying her a visit. The men mostly come out whistling so they figured her evil was never so bad as we told them, and in that they may have been right.

Hester shook her head for Libby. No, she had not been to Sally's.

'Your daddy bring them tears on?' asked tall Sissie Jane, her words tender. I reckon she knew what was starting up, even back then when nothing had happened you could put your finger on.

For answer the child clung closer to Libby's dress.

'Let me in there,' said Sissie as she grabbed Hester away with her long straight lumberjack arms, hauling the girl through the air and onto her own spacious lap. There wasn't too much padding on her thighs, them days or now, but it was a good enough lap for a child, the warm lap of a good soul. It was Sissie Jane as was responsible for the child's existence and like as not she was thinking that very moment she best make the girl's life worth living now she had give it to her. Better leave the babe die inside it's mammy than breathe life into it then cast it aside with no help in the world, that's what I would feel if it was me. And no help coming from Solomon her father and Joe her brother, not as anyone on the outside could see.

Hester resented them arms as stole her away from Libby's rich bosom and she struggled as best she could against the grip of Sissie Jane. She might as well of took on the Lord hisself is the advice I would of give her.

'And we'll start by wiping up them tears,' said Sissie, and you could see the warmth of her flooding up through them thighs as wiry as any man's and into Hester's bony body. Whatever thoughts was floating around in Hester's mind just then, you could see them drifting away, harmless now they was over and Sissie Jane there to take a hold of her. I was jealous of that you see, because I could never have that powerful affect on another being. Sissie just set there and stroked the child's damp hair, glossy black and all beaded with water.

'There now,' she soothed and rocked. 'Ain't nobody gonna mess with Sissie Jane, so all the while I'm looking out for you it's all right, y'hear?'

Hester nodded yes.

'There ain't nothing the Lord and I can't sort. You got that?' said Sissie.

I suppose it was important the child believe it, regardless of the truth of it, but the Lord only knew what sorting out Sissie could miracle up as would have made Hester's life any easier. It was the same for all the young girls back then.

'Did he take a strap to you?' asked Sissie Jane, feeling along Hester's thigh for the welts.

'That ain't the first time this week,' said Libby.

Maybe that the child deserved it, I couldn't help thinking at the time, although I feel different now. You can't always be interfering when a man is bringing up his own child.

Libby wiped the sweat from her eyes with her fat fingers and looked in the direction of Solomon's cabin, saying, 'To my way of thinking, that Solomon is getting to like his forms of correction.' It turns out she had a point.

Hester stiffened and Sissie Jane vowed to take Solomon to task. There was enough such men round these parts was born animals, she said to Libby and me, without good men following their very footsteps. He should have wed again, she said, and she should have seen to it he had. Then we all just set there a while and the spigot dripped like always. It makes a soft sound with each drop landing in the mud below. You hear it? I always found it a soothing sound. I sit for hours on this old bench just listening to the drip. Solomon offered to fix it once but I wouldn't let him.

'You spending too much time without fellow company, young Hester,' Sissie said at last, thinking she could get her out that house more and away from Solomon, 'Why don't you and Mary Ellen share your chores now her mammy has gone away,' she went on. 'With the both of you laundering at one place one day and then scrubbing the floors at the other on the next?'

'Will my daddy take offense,' Hester wanted to know, the tears dried now.

'Not if I ask him first,' said Sissie Jane.

Then I got accused of being more out of sorts that day than usual just because I started up about families having the right to bring up their own without other folks butting in their noses. It led to a debate, for that is the whole point of having the pump set up here with the wood bench next to it, so as we can sort out the world's ills right at the source of it all, the water, that and discussing the ignored wisdom of old women.

Anyhow, the three of us was debating that day, long after Hester skipped away, happy for a while, to where Mary Ellen lived just a few cabins down the track, on the virtues of young mothers leaving their own families to fend as best they could while they lived in as cooks and nannies for white folks. How could you blame the mothers, reckoned Libby, their menfolk with no work, not finding none, nor wanting to, nor able, it came to the same in the end. The women torn between deserting their own families and escaping to life in a clean house with smart clothes and hot water for which the only penalty was slavery again, and white folks trying to shame them. Lesser beings would go and be grateful, washing their hands of the dust and dirt of shanty shacks, unwashed men and empty bellies. But they was wives and mothers and no kind of thinking could will away a bond as left them parted from their own kin, with babes not yet suckled, and hating every minute before they could get back to see them.

*   *   *

True to her word Sissie Jane arranged it so Hester and Mary Ellen shared their chores. Just two days later they was making a game of doing the wash in Solomon's cabin.

'Mary Ellen?' said Hester.

'Yes'm Miss Hester.'

'You done them chores as I set you?' said Hester.

'Yes'm. I done set the bread to rising and the children has had they breakfast,' said Mary Ellen.

'And all the laundering?' Hester wanted to know.

'Yes'm Miss Hester. I has set the whites to boil and am just wringing out these here dungarees.'

'You suggesting my family has a need of dungarees Mary Ellen?' said Hester testily.

They glared at each other. What Hester meant was dungarees smelled of dirt and poverty and their own bleak lives. This was a game, where starched white dresses and clean houses with pretty rugs lived and belonged. Mary Ellen had come close to breaking the game.

'This here's the children's pretty clothes for Sunday churchin,' corrected Mary Ellen, as she held up a pair of men's work trousers from the tub of wash water, a tub so large the child could barely reach into without losing her balance.

16

'With the baby's new romper suit and all?' asked Hester, seeing not the great wood tub but a dainty zinc one like in the advertisement hoardings in town.

'Yes'm, with Young Jeremiah's new blue rompers.'

'Jeremiah never is a white name,' Hester objected again. 'That ain't right. You're spoiling the game.'

Mary Ellen threw down the heavy dungarees into the water and gray suds flew out at them both. She stamped her foot.

'It's me as knows white names, for my mammy is the one caring for the white children.'

Hester left off from the mangling and wiped suds from her face with the inside of her elbow. That was an unfair blow from Mary Ellen, inferring she had a mother where Hester did not.

'Jeremiah is never a white boy's name,' Hester insisted calmly.

'Yes it is so,' said Mary Ellen. 'Jeremiah is just a grand name and when I has a baby boy that is just the name I'm going to give him.'

'Grand it may be,' said Hester hearing Sissie Jane's tone of voice in her own, 'but they calls their boys Billy and Johnny and such.'

'It's my mammy as knows,' Mary Ellen repeated.

'Your mammy may know, but you don't,' said Hester.

'She's tending them right now,' Mary Ellen sulked.

Mary Ellen's mother lived in a different house to raise another, some thought better, family at the expense of her own. She came home just high days and holidays, sending wages to keep her own five children fed, entrusting her love to each envelope. She had sold her family in return for the food to keep them growing. It was a strange kind of growing with so little love available in it.

'It never was no game worth playing,' said Mary Ellen, 'when the snooty lady of the house has to get her hands in the wash tub too.'

'That's just pretending,' claimed Hester. 'I can pretend with the game while I wash the clothes.'

'When I'm playing the grand lady you won't find me acting menial,' said Mary Ellen as she swung the dungarees from the tub to the mangle.

'We won't be a playing the game again if you can't work faster and better. This floor needs mopping now from all the mess. It was laundering at my place and scrubbing at yours. Now we're to do scrubbing all over, looks like.'

They mangled and rinsed and mangled again for over an hour with no further role-playing. They were almost done when Solomon stormed in after an argument with Hester's brother Joe. It seemed Joe had been earning extra on the car repairs and keeping the money for himself. Solomon wanted it handed over, just as the weekly wages were given up each Friday. He came into the house, annoyed with Joe not Hester, but Hester was nearest, and smallest. She was easy to be angry with.

'Whatever is with all the messing here,' he stormed, catching her a swipe that made her lose her balance on the wet floor. 'I told you not to be messing the house when the wash tub can be took out on the porch.'

He pulled her up by the front of her dress, straining the cotton print.

'I tried, we both tried,' whined Hester, her stick limbs flailing on the soapy floor. 'The tub wouldn't get up over the step for all we dragged it,' she moaned.

He looked into her wide eyes then threw her down, sending her flying again.

'Get to mopping,' he yelled. 'You too.' He switched his attack to Mary Ellen who'd been backing her way over to the door. 'You too,' he repeated.

Hester was shamed for her friend but she was also concerned for herself. He wouldn't start on her until Mary Ellen left, so she must keep her friend in the house at all cost. She set to drying the floor and he went over to his chair by the window to clean out his pipe. After he'd moved off, Hester looked up. Mary Ellen was standing near the tub, her hands tight down by her sides clutching two fistfuls of skirt, her mouth open.

Hester nodded towards the pail on the floor and mouthed the message for her to empty the wash water. The last thing Mary Ellen wanted was to stay in the house but she was too timid to walk out on Mr Solomon so she picked up the pail and got on with the emptying. She didn't want one of Hester's waking fits to come on.

There was still a half tub full by the time Hester finished the floor so Mary Ellen tried to hand over the pail, anxious to be away. Hester refused it and set about piling the mounds of wet washing into a basket so it would be ready to take out and dry. She hoped to get the meal warming and then have the two of them escape to the yard to hang the clothes. Reluctantly Mary Ellen went back to the wash water.

It was when Mary Ellen dropped the pail and spilled the water that Solomon leapt up again, his bad humor in no way eased by his pipe smoking at the window. It was Mary Ellen's clumsiness but it was Hester's ear that caught the blow, knocking her against the heavy tub and sending her and the tub skidding halfway to the door. For a moment it seemed the washtub and it's remaining suds would tip and spill. Mary Ellen screamed and ran out as the tub rocked noisily, then Hester clawed her way through the mess of washing, pails and water to follow her out through the door. Solomon kicked out with his boot, trying to slam the door closed before Hester had quite slipped through it, but the door caught her on the back of the shoulder and propelled her even quicker down the porch steps. He swore under his breath then kicked over the tub for good measure. That girl was getting just too big for being treated as a child.

By the time Sissie Jane called round later that evening, to deliver the fruit for a pie and to check the rumor that Solomon's temper was getting out of hand again, Hester was in the other room, pretending sleep.

Solomon hadn't meant to hurt her. Even less had he meant to rip her dress the way he had. He knew how she loved the blue frock and, besides, it was the only one that still fitted her. It would have to be mended now and she would hate to have it patched with something from Sissie Jane's mending box. It was just that the dress was too long, he thought, longer than he expected, and it had covered the part of the legs he was taking the strap to. He hadn't thought it might tear, he just wanted to pull it out the way of the strap, the legs. And her legs were growing so long these days. You had to get a strap to a girl early or there'd be no end of trouble once she started with boys. It was up to a father to get his authority strapped into a girl. It was a known fact.

Solomon smoked his pipe and fingered the buckle on his belt with his free hand as he talked to Sissie Jane of others things, of fruit pies and Joe's car mechanics. He never mentioned the strapping, but she knew anyway. She knew from the guilt in his eye that he was uncomfortable with himself, maybe not with what he had done but with what he had felt. Sissie Jane was a great understander of people and she knew Solomon well enough to know guilt when she saw it. Maybe he had just frightened himself with his own thoughts. She hoped so.

'And it's no worry to you that she looks so like your wife?' asked Sissie

Jane, taking the conversation away from Joe's cars all of a sudden.

Solomon choked his pipe right out of his mouth.

'Hester?' he asked stupidly.

'It's when she turns her head and looks at you from the one side,' said Sissie Jane.

'No. No, it ain't no worry to me, but ... I declare the child's a devil. And there's times ...,' he was careful as he spoke, '... times as I'd wish you to have left her where she lay inside of my wife.'

It was then he placed the pipe onto the window ledge and put his head in his hands and wept in a silent way that took Sissie Jane quite by surprise, making her stand up and mutter something about the fruit pie dish and not bothering to return it until it was convenient and then sending her out the cabin door and into the moonlight. She knew she had to look out for young Hester, but who was to look out for Solomon?

He did it because it had to be done, Solomon told himself again as he gave up waiting for Joe to come home and turned in for the night. It was just he hadn't thought to be so harsh with her this time.

Hester heard them both go to their bed that night, her father first and then her brother Joe, but she kept her eyes tight shut. Both into the big high bed together, her daddy snoring loud by the time Joe crept in just before light. Always before she had wanted to join Joe in that coolness of the big bed under the window, or have him share the trundle bed with her, but she watched the two of them, open mouthed and sleeping noisily together, and knew she would have to remain split away from her only family and continue to sleep alone on the far side of the room.

That night she ran her hands over the strap marks on her backside and knew life had changed. She no longer wanted their company and she thanked God and her dead mother for her own few feet of safety and the quilt to hide under.

Hester watched her brother in sleep. The flames were all around him but only smoldering gently, nothing to frighten her with just yet. She fingered her own sore flesh and a fear went through her, drowning her again where she touched. A bolt shot right through her hand, and then she caught her breath. Another shot went up her arm and her breath would not come even when she tried to pull it in through her mouth. Lungfuls of seawater flooded in to make her head spin but she fought against it because it had happened before and she knew she could fight it. It wasn't about her being born and killing her mother, it was something else. She fought for breath, then, as she ran her fingers across her throat, she felt the water seeping from her mouth, letting her breathe once more. She was still alive, she thought, and whole. It hadn't happened yet. Would it help to tell Sissie Jane when she couldn't explain what it was? It wasn't the one about Joe and the fire, this was her own pain. And for all it had to do with fire, it was more the water that was important. Her choosing the water. She didn't know when it would happen or if it had happened already to the girl in her head.

Hester thought she had stayed awake after Joe came home but she must have drifted into sleep. There was a day in her head, cool she remembered, the air was cool ... cool air wrapping round her thin dress ... and damp. The memory brushed wet on her face and she tasted salt. Chattisham, Hintlesham, people and places. Creeks, not here, not the cricks round these parts, but those off the Blackwater River. Salt. Gray and mud flats. The damp hung over her feet. Why did they say fog swirls when really it hangs? Leaden and weighted, waiting. A deadener of sound. Of names. Chattisham, Hintlesham. All those noises trapped in the heavy mists, hoofsteps, footfalls, voices calling was there anybody there.

Hester shivered in her warm trundle bed, shaking off the remnants of the dream and the wet mist. The sun streamed through the window onto the empty bed, the quilt in a pile on the floor where Joe and her father had left it. It must be late and she should have been up frying the breakfast before the two of them started their work. Why hadn't they called her? She threw back her cover, still feeling the chill, and hunted round for her dress. As she stood in the room, a thin girl with a child's shapeless legs and her white drawers hanging too big round her waist and gaping at the thigh, she saw the ruined blue frock at the foot of the bed. The thought of it was too shameful. It would never be her loved dress again, not even if the tear could be mended so no one would see. Hester picked it up and stuffed it away under her quilt, then searched through her other clothes, holding them against her growing body to find the most decent.

Watching from the pump a few minutes later, Sissie Jane saw Hester clasping her bare arms in her hands and hugging herself warm in the hot sun.

Hester knew when they finally burned her brother she would learn more about the people and places in her head. Very soon they would find Joe dead. Hanging, burned and dead. So many times she had lived his death that she felt, amongst the grieving, there would be a sense of relief. At last it would be over. Maybe she would be able to stop dreaming.

Hester often heard voices in her head but she wasn't to know it was unusual. She thought maybe everyone had another life too, one with a cast of characters that lived a separate time inside your mind. She sat down in the dust outside the cabin, passing time doing nothing more than keeping out of her father's way. Solomon always fretted when he saw her idle.

'Southern trees bear strange fruit,' thought Hester.

'What's that?' asked Joe, her brother.

'Blood on the leaves and blood at the root,' she thought.

'You talking to me?' Joe wanted to know.

'Black bodies swinging in the southern breeze...' Hester hadn't realized she was speaking out loud.

'You have to shout up. I can't hear you over the wireless,' Joe called over from where he was working on the car.

'Strange fruit hanging ... in the poplar trees,' said Hester quietly.

Joe left off working on the engine or carburetor or whatever it was he had been tinkering with and straightened his long back. Shiny back, noticed Hester. Shiny wet back, not a bit like ebony. Why did white folks say that? The wireless was a little way off, not his own of course, not on the wages he got for fixing Mr Clarkson's car or Mr Clarkson's fence or Mr Clarkson's backside for that matter. Hester, go wash your mouth out with soap, she told herself. Where did you hear language the likes of that? What she wanted to think was 'Mr Clarkson's ass' but her mind wouldn't let her think a bad word like that. It settled for 'backside' and knew it had let her down. She was only eight.

Joe cut the wireless, the static blaring to an all-time high just before it faded out.

'Wish you wouldn't mumble so when I is working,' he said, looking over to where she sat, her faded print dress pulled down trying to hide her knees. 'I can't hardly hear what you say, then I has to stop. Sorry Mr Clarkson sir, couldn't get your automobile ready on time like I promised, on account of my little sister mumbling like she does.'

22

He saw the worried look on her face and walked over to where she sat just below the stoop, then he smiled at her a little and ran his fingers over her hair.

'They have grease all on them,' she said and pulled away. But it wasn't the grease that frightened her.

'Joe?' She spoke his name and then paused, waiting just long enough for him to get half back to the car fixing and have to turn around. 'You like poplar trees?' she said at last.

'Not more'n any others,' he said.

Hester watched her brother and wondered why he did that to her, making her see the flames all round him like that? Standing in such a way that it made the fear strike through her. It made her drown when he touched her, his hand shooting a bolt right through her that made her catch her breath. That is what made her draw away, not the grease. It was like the times she recalled as a young girl, playing with the chickens, chasing after them, reaching out for one and getting a shot through her arm, the one that her daddy would kill later for supper. Her breath would not come even though she tried so hard to pull it in through her mouth. Instead the lungfuls of seawater flooded in to make her head spin. She always knew the chicken he would catch next, the one they would have for supper. The red, the speckle, or the one with the touch of black on its wing. The one she would find dead and hanging in the porch for Joe to pluck.

She went back to playing with the insects in the dust for a while, blocking their busy paths with pieces of stick and dry cornhusk, watching their confusion. She never heard the wireless turn back on or saw the men that came for her brother in their white peak hoods. It was the smell she noticed first. The smell choked her, making vomit rise in her throat to meet it. Then she saw Joe's face screaming silent at her through the flames. She never expected it to smell so sweet, she thought. Sickly. Sickening. The fat dripping off him, a festive roast. Sizzling and screaming. The black skin shrinking. Peeling off.

Strange fruit hanging in the poplar trees.

The magnolias were the worst, battling sweetness through the stench of it all. Sweet and fresh. Burning flesh. The heat scorched her own face as she stood beneath him. He screamed, but she could do nothing. There

23

was nothing to be done. They had done everything. There was nothing she could undo. The crows would be there tomorrow. Fruit for crows. To pluck. The rain to gather. Wind to suck. Sun to rot. Tree to drop. Here is a strange and bitter crop.

Then she threw up and became aware from the warm wet on her feet that this was real vomit. Sometimes she had trouble sorting out what was happening now from what would happen later.

'Why ever are you retching up like that?' called Joe from where he worked on the car. 'You sick?' He left off from the car engine a second time.

Joe was still here then, she thought. Had they not done it yet? Would it help to tell him? Did he know already? Did other people know before, as she did? She would have to ask Sissie Jane. Then her daddy Solomon came out on the stoop and wanted to know what was causing such a fuss, telling her not to cry so. And someone at the spigot tut tutted over her screaming, saying it was her being born and killing her mother. Her mother being too old for a child anyroad.

Chapter 2

JOE'S STORY

Old Loula took out some knitting from her string bag and pieced her recollections together with every stitch. The man listened intently, wanting to take notes but unwilling to interrupt the flow of her talking. Old Loula's voice drew such a picture he wondered if he heard more than she said, as if he was painting some of the details into her tale. She certainly was a good storyteller. And he had always been a good listener. That was probably part of the trouble, he thought.

They had been sitting at the seat by the faucet for an hour already and he wanted to get changed into more casual clothes. It had been a long drive and he felt out of place in a business suit; that and the sun was making him sweat. He was also worried about finding a hotel so he was about to excuse himself when the old woman said something that made him stay.

I should tell you about Joe, Old Loula said, Hester's brother. Maybe I should of paid him more mind for he was a good boy in many ways. He was never like the other young men, not that he was queer in the head or anything like that, more that he was quiet. Wouldn't take to socializing, as did the other boys his age. Always more interested in his engines and mechanicking, preferring the silent company of a machine to any criticisms maybe arising from living things, dogs and horses included alongside of men and women. And as for women, well, he was looking to be seventeen that summer and still never talking to a girl much less marrying with one. Not like Libby's Zac, her youngest, just fifteen and a father already as if Libby hadn't enough worries in the world, so she told us all, without little girls' fathers complaining about more children on the way. But that was Zac, like his mother. Never a family to miss out on loving if it was free. Though, like as not he was finding just how costly free gifts can turn out.

Joe was never like that. Young Joey had seen too much that night from under the kitchen table. His mother butchered by the red calico nightdress and a sister hauled into the air. Them telling him it was a baby but him knowing it for another bloodied mess, a part of his mother cut off and waved in the air at him, above the table where he huddled out of sight. Just as an arm or a leg ... a piece of her flesh like Mr Clarkson's pig when it was bled and sectioned into hams ... that's what he knew it was for sure, until it cried out at last. A pathetic bleat to prove to little Joey that his mother was really spent. And Sissie Jane with the blood drenched all over her calico nightdress.

Women were all blood red to Joe, for as long as he could remember, and that was about as far back as he cared to recall, to the day little Hester was cut out his mother. After that he didn't care to get on speaking terms with women for they might just die on you and be hacked up, or be born mewing from someone you loved, or just be covered in red calico. Whatever way, Joey didn't want it.

So little Joey grew up as best he could, the three of us women, Libby, Sissie Jane and me, looking out for him. To Joey it seemed like his pa was irritated all the time at his being in the house, then mad again when he took hisself off to the crick and his pa had to come look for him. Joey learned early that there was no winning. But it was that small creature, the one they called the baby, that upset him most. In the early days the sound of it wailing would send him under the table and fill his eyes with red calico clouds, and he would cry too, the pair of them shrieking enough to send poor Solomon to despair. Not that Solomon gave a moment's wonder as to how any of us women was better equipped to cope than himself. As if the having of breasts, whether milk filled or dry, would bring an order back to his life.

There come a time at last when the new child learnt to keep her hunger and her fears to herself and so the screaming shriveled to a gentle mewing. Then little Joey would creep out from the safety of his table and shuffle near to where the dark legs kicked the air above the laundry basket where they kept her. It was weeks before he touched her, extending his fingers into the basket, feeling the warmth of the air just above her rich brown skin, not dusty as his own from playing in the yard but bathed clean and patted dry by Sissie Jane as he had watched from under the table, not coming out even for the slice of fresh corn bread she would tempt him with. And now the skin so near his fingers he could touch it if he wanted. But he didn't want, in case it might turn red, or be his mother's butchered arm and not a baby at all. That was when the young baby hand first flew up and clenched at one of Joey's fingers. For Joey it stirred something. Some part of him would always hate the thief who stole his mother, yet the warm hand, the tiny grip needing to feel another when for so many hours it kicked and clenched against nothing but thin air. Something started then. A small commitment on his part, to share the loss and help her survive.

From then on he looked out for her, not always liking his charge and never agreeing to love her in any way, yet watching for her. Like the time she crawled to the stove and pulled herself up, the wool of her hair brushing the pot handle before Joey could quite race across the room from where he was shining his pa's boots and take the worst of the scalding bean water on his own arm, pushing her wide of the tipping pan. And when she cried, from fear and the few hot splashes he couldn't prevent, it just wasn't in him to comfort her. That was never part of the deal he made with himself. And so she always felt he hated her, grew up adoring him but never able to get close. The pink scar and the many hidden ones Joe kept to himself.

And there were times the child Hester just blanked out, like she was sleeping, only it happened between lifting a spoon from her bowl of grits and getting it to her mouth. She just stopped. The world went on but she missed that bit, her patch of time being shorter than other folk. There she would be, sitting next to Joey and half way towards a big smile and about to be telling him some new word she had found out how to say, and her eyes would look straight past his head and into the wall. Then he knew to wait the five or ten minutes till she come back. The funny thing was she never knew she was gone and Sissie Jane had told Joey never to make mention of it. Sissie told him those were Hester's time with God and he should respect that and wait for God to be finished with her company. It made him creepy until he was old enough to think it through for himself and decide that was just the kind of thing old ladies told small boys to keep them in their place. But he always knew Hester's smile would snap back and she would carry right on with whatever she was doing before, just as if she never had gone into a waking sleep.

Later they should have been true allies, Joe and Hester, joined against Solomon's anger because Solomon blamed Hester for stealing his wife and little Joey for demanding to be raised and fed when he had no woman to do it for him. But Joe switched camps as soon as he came of a certain age and could defend himself against his father's hands, sometimes hurting with a strap, other times more careful, for his pleasure. Joe was glad to see his sister grow and note his father watching her lengthening legs. She took the strap more now, and not because she was slack or bad with the chores and needed to be chivvied. Joe knew it well. When his father's belt came off it mostly ended another way. Now it was Hester's turn. Joe was happy to switch camps. He watched her legs grow too.

What put an end to his watching was the flames. They tarred Joe, feathered him all over and hung him from a tree.

And it wouldn't be a poplar tree, which would surprise Hester. Maybe surprise is the wrong word for a young girl grieved and shocked, but she had definitely expected a poplar tree. If she could be so certain of his death, picture it all so correctly, how come she could get the tree wrong? It would remain one of the biggest puzzles for her.

It was a plain old afternoon that day before the Klan first came and the old fears hadn't haunted Hester for a while. No smells of Joe's flesh singeing when she went about her daily business, no favored chickens scorching her hands when she stroked them and ending in the cookpot as if she, herself, had sealed their fate. Nothing untoward and Hester had still not got around to confiding the strange voices in her head to Sissie Jane. Joe just took his jacket from the chair in the kitchen and tugged at Hester's hair on his way to the door. She looked up and smiled at him as he tucked his shirt inside the belt of his thick gray pants.

'Don't you hold up supper on account of me,' he said, although he didn't give a reason, which led Hester to wonder if maybe he had a girl he was seeing.

No, she decided, Joe didn't have time for girls.

As it turned out, she was wrong. Joe was as sweet on someone as he was likely to get, but it was forbidden fruit. Finally it would be him being the strange fruit hanging from the poplar trees.

Joe had found himself a girl at last but their relationship went no further than talking. Her name was Charlotte. Joe knew it was trouble from the start. A few weeks before she had seen him delivering Mr Clarkson's car and she had insisted they meet one afternoon. Joe refused of course. He evaded her eyes and refused her suggestions to the point of rudeness, as she pointed out to him.

'You sure are a rude boy,' she teased. 'What is your name?'

'Joe. The name's Joe. And I fixes Mr Clarkson's car on occasion,' he said quickly. 'Ma'am,' he added, lowering his eyes again. And inside his eyelids it wasn't red calico at all. And the fear was different. It stirred him in a way the other girls never had.

'Well Joe, I just think a boy should take the trouble to be polite after a lady has embarrassed herself into addressing him. Ain't that right?'

'Yes ma'am.'

'I was only asking for instruction on the workings of the automobile, a machine I find fascinating,' she drawled.

'Yes ma'am. Ain't nobody in this town can tell you more 'bout engines than what I can,' he stumbled on, still unsure why any pretty woman would be fluttering her eyelashes at him. Not that she was pretty as such. He always had found white women to be lacking in something, though he could never be sure if it was the lean lips or the mean butt he disapproved of.

She had walked with him all the way back to the drugstore where Joe had arranged to meet Clem for a ride back home in his wagon. White folks and black were looking at him by then and he promised to meet her the next day just to put an end to her talking before Clem arrived.

Their conversation, that next day, was very guarded on Joe's part. It was dangerous and he didn't much care for her anyway. Initially she seemed to enjoy the fear in him and she wanted to see more of those bare shoulders that she had so often spied tinkering over the Clarkson car. Mr Clarkson was her uncle, her father's brother. It was on the third meeting, when she finally gave up flirting with him and just coaxed from him his love of engines, that Charlotte Clarkson and Joe began a tentative friendship. She had become bored by young suitors trying to impress her with their rivalries; especially sick of Nathan Clarkson, her cousin, who seemed to take it for granted she would socialize with him and favor him with intimacies at the end of an evening together. In Joe, finally, she had found a friend.

They met most days after that, both aware of the strange effect they had on each other, now a calm pleasure with no playacting, no show, no flirting or teasing. In fact they rarely spoke as they sat and bathed in each other's company. Charlotte might ask a question about how the gearbox worked and Joe would lay out stones and twigs on the ground as he demonstrated the simple mechanics of how one lump of metal would interact with another to produce an effect. He made it understandable and never talked down to her because she was a woman. Neither did he make allowances for her whiteness and show any deference in his manner. Their difference was unspoken but it had ceased to have any relevance to themselves. Sometimes they remained silent for a long time, consumed by the pleasantness of sitting together.

One afternoon Joe and Charlotte sat content by the creek and talked of motorcycles and speed and where they would travel if the world was an easier place and they didn't live in the back of beyond. They didn't sit close. Charlotte had withdrawn her attentions by now and was finding the peacefulness of a shady seat, watching the fish swim, more of a reward. Joe pitched small sticks into the water at intervals and wondered how it could be that sitting here was as tranquil as sitting with Clem. Part of him wanted to be excited by her but he feared to call back the red calico that had haunted him. Better to soak in the scent of her silence and be happy with what he had. He knew by now that he could relive the smell of her in the safety of his bed at night where he could allow it into his head and his imagination. Somehow this was more possible with Solomon snoring beside him to keep the red calico and the red flesh of his women from being cut off and hefted into the air in front of his eyes.

That afternoon it surprised them both when Nathan Clarkson came through the trees running with his hound and nearly mowed Joe down, not expecting to find anyone sitting by the creek in the afternoon sun. You could tell he was shocked by the way he said nothing at all for some time, just stopped dead and looked from Charlotte to Joe and back again. Then he went very red in the face and the redness crept round his ears and down his throat. That was where his anger showed, on his ears and throat. He never said a word that afternoon, just cut a switch from a bush and whistled his dog to heel. Before he was quite out of sight, Joe saw him take the switch to the dog and beat him with it. They could hear the dog yelping through the trees.

That was all really. Joe offered to walk Charlotte back to the road but she was worried for him and said he should get home and stay out of sight for a few days. They agreed not to meet, and they meant not to, but that wasn't how it worked out.

Joe told himself he wasn't scared. All the way home he said it over in his head, but it wasn't true. He ran through the low trees, knocking branches out of his way and trying to whistle as if it was no big deal. As if the Clarksons weren't Klan, when everyone knew they were, because most of the town was Klan. As if it wasn't even his own fault, which it was. He had set the trap himself, he knew. Joe stopped whistling and kicked out at a tree, a magnolia.

'Shit!' he said aloud.

A brown puppy had wandered over from Sally's to check out the noise and now he whined, guilty, assuming the curse was intended for him.

'It's okay for you fella,' Joe addressed the pup, 'dog class ain't judged on color.'

He presumed he was right be he wasn't too certain. Maybe there was a hierarchy amongst dogs he didn't know of.

The puppy yelped again, then wagged, then spiraled, chasing his tail before collapsing on the dust dry leaves and setting to the dutiful task of licking his parts. Joe thought about his own and got real scared then. He had heard things.

He set off again, getting near to home now, and tried to make sense of it all, of his feelings, why he had talked to Charlotte in the first place and why he still wanted to see her again now, even more urgently than before. He broke into the clearing by Libby's cabin and the water spigot was just a short way off, he could see it almost. He ran, getting himself hot to disguise the sweat that stood out on his back and was soaking through his shirt. His long legs pumped the hard ground and scattered the chickens that always congregated at the spigot the same as the old biddies.

'Shoo,' he shouted at one, an old scraggy bird, that refused to move fast enough and nearly went under his boots. As it was he veered to one side of it, tripped and all but fell.

'Sweet Jesus,' he muttered.

He tried to act normal as he came up to their own cabin, keeping the outside show safe with swearing at chickens and forming conversations in his head about Mr Clarkson needing some new tires to replace the worn ones at the front. It never stopped the other side of his brain from running through the possibilities; should he leave tonight, or maybe just announce his future departure for some big city, making sure the Clarksons got to

31

know of it and hope that would be enough. Or he could carry on and enjoy the company of the first woman that ever made him feel right since his mother died. Number three just kept coming to the top of the pile.

Are you as stupid as folks always say, he asked himself, silently, inside his head, as he took the porch steps two at a time and bounded through the screen door. You are a great moron, he told himself as he strode through the porch and into the cabin. It seemed his mind was made up.

'Have to get them front tires switched to the back of Mr Clarkson's car and get new ordered for the front,' he announced to Solomon and Hester who both looked up, Hester from the stove and Solomon from his chair by the window.

'You ran all the way to tell us that, boy?' asked Solomon.

Hester got a queer feeling in the pit of her stomach.

Not much else was said though it was plain as day something was up. It was later in the evening, at supper that the first warning came. One of Mr Clarkson's boys called out from the clearing for Joe to come out because there was a problem with the car and he was needed real quick. Joe was out the chair and across the room, scattering fork, grits and his share of bread, long before the shout was half out the boy's lips.

That night it was a warning only. There were two men on horseback and six or seven on foot, all in their hoods and robes, and Joe got off lightly with a cut eye, a few ribs bruised and a directive to leave town. One of the horse riders had a thick leather belt nailed to a baseball bat and he got off his horse and went after Joe until the thickset one on the gray horse called him to wait. There was still some light in the sky when they set on him, enough for folk to see if they dared to, but who would dare? Those in white had nothing to fear for they were the law. Then they all turned and left except the one with the baseball bat who was loath to go and dragged behind. Joe knew it was Nathan by his shoes and the way his feet turned in, and those were his trousers showing beneath the robe. Besides, he had the sleeves turned up for the summer heat and he could see the check of his shirt, the wristwatch and those hands of his. Those hands had been on Charlotte, he thought. He looked again to check as the man got back on his horse. It was Nathan all right. You either knew someone or you didn't. Wearing white was no disguise. More of a threat.

Panic rippled round the cabins after that. A silent unspoken panic that was never quite on anyone's lips for all that it spread like gossip the next day. Sissie Jane, as always the first to act, went over early and insisted Hester come stay with her for a few days, refusing all protestations from Solomon and claiming she was having a bit of a turn herself and needed Hester to look out for her until her dizzy spells wore off. Sissie Jane was known for dizzy spells that could manifest themselves whenever she needed them.

Hester tried refusing, standing in the corner of the room by the stove with one bare foot rubbing up the back of her leg and looking just like stork. Her hand went up to twist a plait of hair as the rest of her body wriggled in protest but that was when her brother picked her right up and threw her over his shoulder, making it a game and carrying her halfway to the spigot before she insisted she had at least to take some clean drawers and a comb with her if she was going on a visit. She and Sissie Jane then collected her things into a basket which Sissie carried while Joe took turns with piggybacks and walking her, for which he held her hand. It was unusual for Hester and Joe to be so close.

Sissie Jane's cabin was the furthest away from the spigot and, in truth, it would have been nearer for her to go the other direction for water where there was a well some other folks used. But she was never one for taking the easy road and she also knew what things were important in life. These were her people, not the folks at the well. That was just how life was.

When they were about half way through the trees, getting quite a way down the path towards the cabin, Joe felt Hester's thin arms go tight around his neck and her legs tense where she sat piggyback inside the cradle of his locked arms. She was having one of her waking sleeps. She had done it more as a young child, less now, going rigid and losing touch for a few minutes. Like falling asleep but she would do it standing or sitting and never fall over, not even close her eyes. She just blanked off. He felt her now and though he'd been about to put her down for a spell he decided to carry her further. Something about her helpless on his back made him imagine Sissie Jane running back along this path in the dead of night with his pa panting to keep up, both of them racing to butcher his mother and haul Hester into the world. The red calico came back to him as it always did but this time he saw the picture from outside of himself, as an outsider, not the blinkered view he knew from under the table. He saw Sissie's long straight legs as she ran through the trees, longer than his own even now, pumping into the ground and her pure white shift flying away from her legs in the moonlight. A part of him shivered then to realize he could see the fine detail of the hairs on her legs when he knew he was seeing nothing but his imagination. Even that thought didn't interrupt the flow of images. He saw her then, striding towards his mother, pulling back the red covers and reaching for the still warm belly. He watched Sissie Jane turn her head and he saw himself cowering under the table.

Hester fidgeted on his back and they both shivered. Joe wondered what in hell brought that on, like a nightmare only he was still awake. That was when Hester bent over one shoulder and kissed his ear all wet and warm. There never had been much affection shown between them and it was strange to have it now after all this time.

'Sorry Joe,' she said as she squeezed her arms tight around his neck.

'I should rightly think you are sorry young Hester, making my ear all wet like that. That's worse than when Sally's dog puppy comes slavering at me.'

But secretly he was pleased, if puzzled. The nightmare of Hester's birth had always played in his head as his own limited view from under the kitchen wood table. He wondered if the same images had been playing through Hester's head, of Sissie Jane being called out for her birth. Joe felt her body relax now that the day sleep moment had passed, but he wondered if they always gave her dream times like the one he had just picked up.

* * *

By that same evening, just twenty-four hours after the first warning, Joe was desperate to see Charlotte again. He persuaded himself it would be the last time, that he would walk the miles into town to tell her just that. There was to be no more meetings, he would say, and he was set to leave town in a few days. He repeated all this to himself several times as he wandered round and round the empty cabin before he set off. Solomon was out.

Maybe he should pack a bag and leave right after seeing her, Joe wondered. He would be safer with a packed bag in case he ran into them on the way. 'See guys? I'm packed and on my way. Joe's leaving town just like you said.' That was it, he thought. Pack now and go. It was a good idea. He strode into the bedroom and threw shirts, a towel, his other pants and a razor into a pile on the mat. Then he dived under the bed for Solomon's cardboard suitcase but when he pulled it out the damp had turned it green and it was almost in pieces. He threw the case into the corner of the room and the dried mildew spores flew up in clouds. Paper, he thought, he could package his belongings in a brown paper parcel. That would work.

His actions were getting more frantic now and he pulled Hester's trundle bed away from the wall, looking for the treasures he knew she kept there, wrapped in paper parcels.

When he saw the neatness of her possessions, a pitiful pile of small boxes and string-wrapped packages, his mother's sewing box and her patchwork material, he knew he couldn't leave Hester behind. He had never even liked the kid, but she was all that remained of his mother. One stupid kid that drove him demented with her stupid childish ways and a few boxes of buttons and ribbons. That was his inheritance. He looked back at the bed he shared with Solomon and knew just how much she needed him. For years he had pictured himself free of Solomon, dreamed of shaking Hester off his back and just striding out of this life and onto a better one. Only now he realized he couldn't leave her to fend for herself. Maybe if he had to go he would take her along, he thought. She would annoy the hell out of him, that was for sure, but some of the resentment he had always felt towards her had faded this morning on the trip to Sissie Jane's.

The long walk to town would be enough to puzzle it out, he decided. Plenty of time to plan if and where they could go. He always thought better when he was walking, he knew, so he abandoned his own small pile of clothing and set off to tell Charlotte that it was all over. Not that it had ever really begun.

*   *   *

That evening in the white part of town, Mrs Clarkson did as a good wife should and set to her part of the work. She had a husband and many fine sons and there were whites needed for all of them. There were display days as well as workdays and those Klan whites got just as messed up on a regular meeting night as they did on parade. For all they came back on occasion with lampblack on the sleeves and thorn rips at the hem it was still the same degree of boiling, starching and pressing with a hot iron. There were days she wondered why they never chose black instead of white. Of course, she could have left them out for Prissy to do of a Monday, with the wash, but Mrs Clarkson did not see that was one hundred percent American somehow. There were certain things as shouldn't be tainted. Some parts of life in this town were, and should remain, sacred.

While Mrs Clarkson was fussing over the pressing of the hoods, the younger Clarksons were putting together a mixture of turpentine, tar and lampblack. They had a special pot kept in the garage for such potions and, in their minds, the pot was not used anywhere near often enough to keep America a fit place to live.

* * *

It was no good, thought Joe. It seemed as stupid to him as it did to everyone else but he just couldn't help it. He wanted to be there, talking to Charlotte, more than anything in the world. The thought of not seeing her again was too much for him to take in. All the words he practiced on the walk just disappeared into thin air when he saw her. Neither said a thing but just looked at the other for a long time. There was no talk of motor cars or all the other conversations they had shared before in the afternoon sun. All of a sudden it was serious. Joe put out his hand towards her, thinking it would be the first time their bodies had touched. He couldn't recall them even brushing against each other before, he had been most careful about that. His hand stayed out like that, alone, for a long while. Would she take his hand? He waited.

Charlotte lowered her eyes and raised them again slowly. Then she stretched out her hand and cupped it under his chin before she pulled his face towards her and kissed his lips. The blood pumped through Joe's forehead so strong he thought his head would burst.

'Charlotte...' He couldn't manage anything else.

'We could go away,' she said.

No, he thought. The woman was crazy. There was nowhere safe for them.

'We could go north,' she added.

Joe had heard of the north pole but he didn't believe that would be far enough. He shook his head, trying to think straight. That was when she kissed him again. Jesus. He had to get away. How could she do this to him and let him know how it might have been? He couldn't stand it. She was running her fingers over him now. Hesitantly he took both her hands in his and begged her to stop.

'No,' he said 'I'm going away. Tonight. Alone. Maybe alone. I don't know about my sister yet.'

'You can't leave me here,' she started. 'My uncle, my cousins...'

'Will they treat you bad?' he wanted to know.

'They said they'd lock me up. Or send me away,' said Charlotte.

'Your own folk would do that?' he asked.

'The folks in town stared at me.'

'I didn't mean for this to happen.'

'Me neither,' she agreed.

'We never should have...' he started.

'But we didn't. We never did anything wrong Joe. I tried ... I shouldn't have. I tried but ... then I found how much I like you.'

They looked at each other. Joe knew he had to leave then, before he took her in his arms. He was hot for her. Hot in a way he never had been when they sat together, alone by the creek. Now he ached. His balls talked sweet nonsense to his brain, making it false promises, telling how everything would be all right if only he could hold Charlotte and show her how much all of Joe cared.

'Who's there?' rasped a voice a short distance away.

It was dark all around where they stood under the bridge. Shadows cut long from the trees in the faint moonlight but it was difficult to see where the voice came from. Quickly Joe pulled Charlotte further into the shadows, making her crouch low where the wooden bridge supports dug into the bank. He had his back against the earth bank and pulled her towards him. Her body was so close he thought the scent of her would make him faint. His heart was pounding so loud it nearly deafened him. Soon he would burst, he knew. He pressed two fingertips gently against her mouth.

'Shh,' he begged.

'Someone there?' said the voice again. A man's voice, gruff, middle-aged. 'I saw you. You young folks didn't ought to be out this late. Decent folks'd be in their homes by now.'

Footsteps started down the bank. They could both hear the crash of sticks and the movement of loose stones.

'I'll get up on the bridge,' whispered Charlotte, 'you wait till I've walked off then head out quick do you hear?'

'No.'

'It's okay,' she mouthed wet lips against his ear, allowing the weight of her body to fall against him. 'I know who it is. He works with my uncle. He can walk me home.'

Joe still had a hold of her arms. He didn't want to leave it like this. He was torn between passion and fear.

'I'm coming down there,' boomed the voice again, 'and if I sees young folk misbehaving I'm after calling the sheriff.'

Charlotte shook herself free, left a damp kiss on Joe's lips and scampered up the incline.

'Don't you be worrying Mr Grant ... it's just me, Charlotte.'

'Charlotte?' repeated the voice in the dark.

'Yes sir. I was just after taking a walk, what with the air so humid these nights I can't hardly sleep unless I've had a good walk to tire me some.'

Charlotte reached the path at the top of the bank just as Mr Grant walked into a patch of moonlight. Lee Grant ran the local paper, the Evening Standard, and he knew Charlotte's family.

'Well I'll ...' he said.

'I would be much obliged for the company,' said Charlotte as Mr Grant moistened his lips and proffered her his arm, 'for you never can be too sure who you might meet on a dark night such as this.'

That was the last time Joe was to see Charlotte.

It was the last time anyone else would see her alive.

* * *

Joe stayed under the bridge and listened. He could smell the scent of her on him. It was on his clothes, his hands. For the first time he was truly intoxicated by her and he wasn't sure how to deal with the new feelings. He waited until their voices died away, Charlotte's charming the old man, Mr Grant's torn between lecturing a young girl for being out alone so late and making conversation with her. Joe stayed pressed against the bank and kept breathing her in, his head spinning with her scent and with the frightening possibilities of leaving town with and without her. Finally he crawled out and started running for home, still unsure what he was going to do when he got there. He needed to run, to feel his feet pounding and his blood thumping because holding Charlotte so close had fired an energy right through his body, unleashing the natural reactions that had for so long been kept in check by the red calico.

He took the creek route rather than the road. You had to know the way well to take it in the dark. When he got to the trees he crashed through the woods, smashing his energy out through them, ripping leaves from their stems and branches from the boughs, his arms waving wildly above his head. It was a long way but seemed to take no time at all. He tried to think, because he knew he had to leave town right away, but thinking was difficult at a time when his hormones had at last decided to race. Get out, yes, he thought with difficulty, that's what he had to do. Leave Charlotte before he changed his mind, rather than drag her into it; Charlotte, the woman he loved. No way was he dragging her into this. But by now he was confused between love and lust.

That was when he saw the light on in Sally's place. For the first time he wished she would stand on her porch as she always did, in that chemise you could see clear through to her dangling breasts and the swell of her rump. He used to watch as a kid, together with Tom and Jimmy, them sitting in the trees and Sally showing her titties to the men that came through the creek. She was old then, he thought, forty maybe.

And the times she had called to him these last years, telling him how she watched his back with his shirt off, how she liked to see the big, strong boy he had grown into, how she was just itching to check out if his thighs and buns were as iron tight as his arms and chest. Well now, just now, if she was to come out on that porch ... he stopped still and waited, willing her and her sagging tits to come into the light from the window. He had no money anyhow, he thought, and made to go back to the path, but his own passion, dormant for so long, frightened him. He suddenly realized it was Sally, or Charlotte the woman he loved, and that must never happen. He didn't ought to feel like this about the woman he loved.

He waited again, thinking the porch light would come on, as it always had, that Sally would walk that long, slow, delicious walk back and forth across the verandah boards, walking the bounds of her property. But she never came out. He must have been there ten minutes already when a wet muzzle snuffled into his leg and nearly frightened the life out of him. It was Sally's brown dog puppy.

'Hey little fella. You had me shit scared there,' said Joe.

The pup rolled on its back; waiting for its belly to be scratched but all Joe could think of was his own ache.

At last he struck out from the creek path and crossed to Sally's fenced yard, the pup following him. The place was better than any of the other cabins, a pretty yard fenced in with a gate and the garden tended to regularly by a short, round man who lived in a town some distance away. The house itself was big with the porch on two sides like an L shape.

Joe was striding towards the porch screen door when it struck him she might have a visitor. He stopped dead. His brain couldn't work out how that would affect him. Would he wait? Was that vile, to take his turn like that, or did it excite him more? Was there a difference between a visitor of five minutes before or the day before? He didn't know how to feel. It was all too new. Even to want a woman was such a novelty he was determined to keep his head from dwelling on it in case it stopped. He didn't want it to stop.

He thought he would sneak to the window that was open at the far side and check it out. When he got there the window was high but as he pulled over a pail to stand on, the puppy yelped.

'Shhh!' said Joe, bending to quiet him, and it was just as he got his footing and hauled himself upright that he came nose high to Sally's breasts on the window ledge.

'Hi,' she said slowly. 'I waited a long time for you, boy. Joseph ain't it?'

He gulped air as he tried to say yes. There was no chemise today, just a silky wrapper tied so loose it had trouble containing the flesh of her breasts, so much bigger than he remembered and just resting on the wood sill, the dark shadow running between them and down, down forever it seemed.

'You coming in?' asked Sally.

He tried again to say yes and wanted to mention the money, that he had none, but there wasn't time. She hoisted herself off the window ledge and disappeared into another room. The door closed behind her and he was left dangling on one foot on a new white enamel pail. The piping of dark blue round the base and the rim reminded him of Old Loula's chipped pail. But hers was never as grand as this one, he thought.

All the way to the porch he tried phrasing about the money. The price scared him because it was unknown. He would tell her he had no cash on him but there was a little of his car fixing money stashed away and he could bring that right back. After that he could pay off in installments.

At last he came to the porch and walked in. Sally was standing in what turned out to be the hallway. There was a kitchen just off to the right and a door closed to the left. The hall passage ran back behind her. Joe's thoughts of the grandness of the house almost took over from the sight of her. Most cabins he had known were two roomers, one bedroom and a room where everything else went on, cooking, eating, living.

'Why aren't you paying me any attention young Joseph,' she asked softly, 'don't you like what you see?'

'The money.' he stammered.

'This one is on the house,' she replied. 'For the next one you can tend my garden.'

Stupidly he waved his arm toward the front of the house, haggling in his own mind about the price of the evening, knowing the stocky, bald guy did her gardening. She stopped him before a word passed his lips.

'I always thought a vegetable garden would be nice,' she said, 'at the back.'

She had a good way of talking. Southern, but the words were gentle and husky not drawled and brash like most folks. She was not from round there.

Finally, he looked at her. The wrapper was the softest material he had ever seen. It clung to her breasts showing him the beautiful roundness of their hang, so low that the tie at her waist pulled the wrapper in tight but was itself hidden. Her hips were not so wide but her butt jutted out

in that teasing way behind making a shelf you could eat your supper off.
He swallowed hard and wondered where such thoughts had come from.
The material needed to cover her behind had pulled at the join in the
wrapper and Joe tried to imagine he could see black tufts of hair down
there, below the round of her belly, but maybe it was just the dark band
of material that edged the wrapper.

Very gently she took his hand and led him down the passageway and
into the bedroom. With every step of her swaying hips he wondered what
he would do when they got there.

She shut the bedroom door behind them and then lit a lamp, not the
kerosene lamps of the cabins but a crystal affair with pink fluid in the
glass. He looked round at the room while she looked at him.

It was like a palace to him. Used to the bare utility of all the cabins
and having sneaked a good look at the Clarkson's home where their idea
of style meant sterile, functional items like big refrigerators, washing
machines and living rooms stripped naked of anything except angled
furniture and bare coffee tables, Joe found himself in Aladdin's cave. Here
there were many small tables but all were cluttered with scent bottles,
leather bound books, statues, glasses, figurines, things so foreign he had
no idea of their function or worth except that they flooded the room
with life. Every wall was a cluttered display, some of paintings and prints,
others of drapes, silk carpets and giant fans. The wall by the window
had masks, African masks. The chairs that lay about the room, waiting
for bodies to sink into them, were cushioned and pillowed and where the
upholstery was old and thin, great tasseled shawls were thrown in a mass
of patterns and colors. To him it was all richness far greater than Mr
Clarkson could ever have furnished.

Sally fingered the buttons of his shirt undone and lowered it to the
floor before smoothing her hands over his rich skin. He was dark, darker
than the high yellow of her own skin. She loved his darkness. Then she
sat him on the bed and wanted him to take off his boots and pants. It
wasn't that she spoke. She just looked at his clothes and he knew what
she wanted. Sally made it all seem simple. Did she know how scared he
was? Could she see his heart pounding through his skin as he stripped off
his clothes?

She kept the light full up while he undressed and he wanted to be
embarrassed when finally he sat there, buck-naked on the bed, but her

eyes wouldn't let him. They brushed every part of him and then her lips joined in, just pursing together and murmuring, but they were telling him he was okay, that she wanted to see his nakedness. She pulled him from the bed and moved him slowly, inspecting him, raising an arm and kissing the skin, turning him gently and smoothing his butt with electric fingers. Now his only fear was that he would come.

Until then he had done nothing, made no move, no touch. He wondered if she would take off the wrapper or would he?

'There is plenty of time,' she said slowly, reading his thoughts. 'Sally has few pleasures for herself in this life. You will be one.'

As she turned to dim the light he thought of other women, women that had touched his life with red, women he could turn red with his power, something he had never wished to piece together as a whole thought but it had to do with them dying if he gave them a child. Red calico. But Sally wasn't a real woman, not a woman like his mother or Charlotte. His sexuality couldn't hurt her could it? He prayed for the red calico to stay away just a while longer but he knew it couldn't and the wilting weakness between his legs made him panic.

'That's better,' said Sally, noticing, 'I want this to take a long, long time. Now,' she pulled at the tie on her wrapper as she flickered her tongue over her lips, 'neither of us will be disappointed ... I promise you.'

But she doesn't know about the calico, thought Joe.

'Sally always keeps a promise,' she said, deliciously slowly as she let her wrapper fall to the floor, 'and you trust Sally don't you?'

He could do no more than nod yes, his willingness to trust, because her wrapper had exposed to him his first truly naked woman.

He had known she was old but that hadn't worried him. He had come to her tonight with one purpose and that was to keep away from Charlotte. He'd waited 17 years to be interested by a woman, had sat with Tom and Jimmy watching Sally's porch at the age of 10 and joined in with their whoops and yelps but nothing had stirred where it should have. There were many that thought he had a liking for men, he knew that, but it wasn't true. Sally was old when he was a kid so he never expected to be excited by her body. Interested maybe, fascinated to discover a woman's body, to explore the difference, desperate to quell this late heaviness in his loins that had caught him defenseless ... but he found Sally was beautiful.

Her breasts hung as huge pendulums, swinging even as she breathed ... low, oh, so low. He wanted to run out and tell the girlie magazines they had it wrong. The pin-up Tom kept in the box under his bed of a skinny girl in a bathing suit was all wrong. Here were breasts. These were breasts. The nipples big and dark, standing out like drawer knobs, and the ring round each one standing guard over all that mountain of flesh. He wanted to touch them, put his face against them, bury himself in the darkness between them.

He wasn't sure how it happened, if she stepped towards him or he went to her but quite suddenly he felt the soft warmth of a teat in his mouth. He sucked and he sucked, slavering, slobbering, he hands molding the mounds of her ass in his fingers. Now his nose was exploring her chest, digging itself a path to the underneath of her breasts, leaving them heavy on his cheeks and muffling his ears.

His hands followed the cleft between her cheeks and explored. The soft puckered skin of her ass amused him for a while and he rubbed it so gently his own ass ached and the skin of his balls tightened even further until he nearly came. If he pushed his fingers just a little further ... it was moist, and soft, and warmer than any place he could imagine.

His body was slipping down her now, mouthing the soft ripples of her belly and the top of his head banging against her great teats at the same time. He was half on his knees, half crouched, his prick hard and crashing against his own thigh when he brought his hands around the front and found that promised thatch of cool dark hair. It was so good there he almost lingered, but one finger fell in, fell right off the cool, dry mound of hair into the crack of wetness beneath. Her lips opened up like a curtain at a theater show. The outer curtains heavy, black, moquette, but they parted in the middle and when pulled aside it was all soft, pale wetness. Silky, that was it. The wetness was silky, oily, like you could spread it all over your skin and rub it in, massage it, oil-like ... not wetness.

Oh ... he had just found the real inner curtains, the gauzy, floating ones ... muslin, gossamer. She shivered as he touched and he knew to be very gentle, to brush like a breeze with his fingers, to pretend they were there traveling past on a route for someplace else and it was only the breath from their passage that she should feel. He knew he was on precious property, hallowed ground, and he would not trespass.

They staggered, clenched together, back to the bed and she found his ear and whispered to him.

'It won't matter if you come. You will come and come, many times before I let you sleep tonight. There will be plenty of time.'

Old Sally was right, of course, and his only lasting thought was to wonder why the Sally's of the world had been looked down on since the times of the bible when it was obvious that they were the mothers of the earth.

Chapter 3

RECALLING 1955 - POPLAR TREES

Loula sat back on the bench and closed her eyes, recalling a time she would rather forget. It was Lee Grant the editor of the newspaper as killed Charlotte, of course, she said, but Joe always got the blame. I never did like that Lee Grant nor his newspaper neither. Old Loula's nose wrinkled as she spoke but she went on. He probably had intended to mention about seeing Charlotte and Joe together under the bridge, to lead the trail away from hisself, but it turned out he had no need to. It seemed most white folks had wind of the affair already and they was more than happy to see it as a cut and dried case.

They found Charlotte's body next morning. It was not a pretty sight apparently and even the sheriff puked when he saw it. The doctor declared rape had taken place before the murder and that was all the proof the town folk needed to be sure it was Joe. In less than twenty-four hours Joe was tried and found guilty by every bit of rumor you can get in a small town.

And if Hester hadn't gone back to the cabin to fetch and return my fruit pan she would never have been wandering down past that way at all, down where the men folk was beating at the sparks on the ground and the bushes, trying to keep the fire from spreading. Down where the shouts of the men for someone to cut him down out that tree was never quite drowned or muffled, it seems, by the women's hands clasped over her ears.

It was a horrid sight I wish never to see repeated and Hester was not the only one cut to the quick that day. By rights, you see, Joe should have been my own boy child if I had just married with Solomon as I might have done. Still, this here is not my story; it is Hester's so I must keep my thoughts to myself. That day is not a easy one for me to recall. Some shouted instructions to cut the rope, others to fetch and throw water from the crick. I just begged outright that he be dead already.

* * *

And much as the women's aprons tried to bury her head and shut out that sight, still Hester saw the flames leaping from Joe's body. The picture was etched inside her eyelids after that. Strangely, it was easier to bear than the one she saw in her head so many times before. But it was only the smell that was exactly right. The tree not being a poplar ... the men folk thrashing around beating flames with their jackets ... none of that fitted with the quiet dignity of her expectations, but the smell was unmistakable. Sweet. Sickly. Sickening. The fat dripping off him, a festive roast. Sizzling. The black skin shrunk back and peeled off. Someone should have added sage or thyme to soften that sweetness. You didn't want magnolias at a time like that. It wasn't right.

The more she tried to breathe the more the seawater flooded into her until her head span with it all. Then Hester threw up over someone's shoes.

There was a thump as Joe's body finally fell to the ground, the rope cut at last, and Hester would have lived the next years easier if she hadn't thought she heard a small moan come from him then.

'He came to set the captives free, Luke 4:18,' said a low voice that might have been Sissie Jane's.

Hester knew she was drowning. She kept pulling at deep lungfuls of air. Yet the air wasn't there - only brack seawater. She knew as surely as she had seen Joe's death so many times before that she herself was drowning. Watching Joe finally tarred and smoking in the tree as she had seen him so many times in her mind, Hester decided she needed to understand the thoughts in her head if she was ever to be free of them.

Someone was trying to take the fruit pan from her that she clutched to her chest, all splashed with vomit.

'Come on Hester,' said another, 'come home now.'

She was still trying to breathe but someone guided her away, the fruit pan was taken off her and the vomit wiped from her mouth with someone's apron. All she wanted was to understand about the poplar tree, the water and the thoughts in her head. Libby said once about everything that was ever known being in a book someplace. Hester knew if she was ever to learn of those things in her head maybe she had to find out from books. Could books tell her about the voices, the feeling she was more than just herself? That another girl lived in her head too? Somewhere maybe there was a book that could explain it all. But there were precious few folks in those parts that knew how to read.

Later that night huddled under the thin quilt on her trundle bed she tried to work it out again. Everyone thought she had closed herself off from grief, after seeing Joe strung up like that, but Hester was planning. She wanted to know how she could learn to read. First she would go to Sissie Jane, she decided, to tell her about the seawater, her drowning, things she felt sure had happened already; not recent but a long time ago. History they called it when it was a time before everyone around you was born. She'd heard about history, it was on Mr Clarkson's car radio program in the afternoons, for schools to listen.

She stopped herself. It was clear she had a muddle here someplace, not knowing which things had happened and which was yet to come. She had known of Joe hanging there charred and smoking with the same pictures that she saw the girl, herself, in some history place. So how could Joe's death be history when she had known it would happen since she was first able to walk? Maybe she, or the girl in her head, hadn't drowned yet? Hester looked at her hands. They seemed the wrong color. How could she tell Sissie Jane she was the wrong color? No, that was silly when you spoke it out loud. Books, she thought. Books would tell her. She had to know more before she could let on to Sissie Jane.

Chapter 4

It was getting late and the man asked about the hotel. Old Loula told him where to find the town but said she had never heard about a hotel so perhaps he should go while it was still light enough to see. She said she would meet him again the next day if he called before lunch. He wanted to fix a time but she didn't seem to work to such a precise system. Before lunch, she repeated, and he had to be content with that. How will I know where to find you, he asked. By the water spigot, was the answer she gave him. He wanted to know about Hester too. Was she still there? Could he meet her? By and by, said Old Loula.

He did find the hotel. It was comfortable enough and more modern than he had hoped so he took the only double king-size room they had and set up his laptop on the small table by the window. It would be more than good enough, he decided. The only thing he should have brought with him was a tape recorder but he couldn't imagine the old woman would be comfortable with it anyway.

* * *

The next day he drove back to the same spot around eleven and parked the car as before. He was looking forward to the day. With a light pair of slacks and an open shirt he would be more comfortable. This time he carried his small leather case with him.

Old Loula was sitting at the faucet waiting for him and he had barely said good day before she launched into the story again. She started where she had left off. I didn't tell you all I should have about Sally, she said. The man sat down, immediately interested.

I'm still in two minds about the woman, said Old Loula, on account of her profession, but these days I see less harm in it than before. The world was a different place then and we had to scorn her, everyone said so. For my part it was there but for the grace of God goes I, I suppose, and maybe that is what made me so self-righteous.

Anyhow, that evening, the same day as they killed Joe, Sally was setting out on her porch none the wiser. No one ran to tell Sally about Joe being dead and strung up in a tree because no decent folk would own to visiting

Sally's place down by the creek so it took a little time for the news to reach her.

It was like most jobs, Sally always reckoned. There was good days and bad and if you expected a ratio of around one to thirty satisfactory to awful you didn't do so bad. From the way most men talked about factory jobs in town even that was doing okay, and she knew from us cabin women that many never saw a good day from one year's end to another. On that basis she didn't do half bad herself. Anyhow, Sally never had reason to regret her profession. And she was her own boss. She never doubted her own decision to allow her only employee, herself, a treat on occasion. It was almost a necessity if she was to remember what in hell about sex was supposed to be worth having. If she lost sight of that altogether then what use was she to her customers? They mostly had wives as could give them that kind of loving. On occasion she had to be reminded herself if she was to earn a living. Research, she called it.

Research was a working code Sally discovered many years before, hence the Gardener. She called him that because that's what he called hisself. In the early years he talked of leaving his wife for the love of Sally but that just made her angry. What good was a husband to her? Loving was a special thing far too precious to be promised on a permanent basis. His every visit was as special as a courting gent's and he tended her flowers for, oh, it would make her smile to work it out and find it was close to twenty years. And he knew there was no need to keep the garden for her. He just did it for kindness.

They still spent such sacred time together. As often as not they sat drinking coffee and playing a hand of cards, and not getting to the bedroom after all. But she never felt like a thief, as if she robbed his wife. No. She only served to teach him the value of love, real love not sex, and sent him back to her a contented husband. The oldest profession, she mused, keeping the bugga man out of little boy's dreams. Old, bald, wrinkled boy's dreams.

It had been a while now since she had done a spot of research. Quite a while, waiting for Joseph to make up his mind. But she knew he would come by in the end. And she knew she would enjoy him. She had thought of his sleek black shoulders and tight belly many times as her fingers had played over the sagging, gray, whiskered skin of her customers. And she knew no other woman would get to him first and spoil him for her. Sally had been watching Joseph for a long time.

She got up from her seat on the porch where she was watching the sun go down. She loved that time, looking out at the swamp and the trees, watching the bugs fly, hearing the birds. She knew some young boys were up in those trees watching her house, waiting for her to light the porch lamp as she always did. They weren't no more than ten years old any of them. Bless'm, she thought. It was always up to Sally to teach them what their folks kept guilty secrets of. They too would grow and marry and dream, dream of Sally's silk chemise in the lamplight as they made love in the dark to their shy wives in white calico.

Sally checked her hair first, in the small hand mirror she kept on the porch table, then she smoothed the chemise over her sagging breasts before lighting the porch lamp. Whyever did men presume it was the shape of a woman's body that turned them on? It was never that. If it was that, then whyever did great fat mamas send a man near crazy with lust and skinny-assed pretty creature bitches make a man turn over, sigh and look for sleep? It was, and always had been, a silent scent that a willing woman put out to the man of her choice. In some professions that scent was manufactured, and that just went to show the skill involved.

Sally started her slow walk along the L shape of her porch, as aware and proud of the effect of her ample body as any prima ballerina on stage. Like footlights her lamp was lit and the outside world became invisible to her.

*   *   *

That was before she got the news about Joe. Sally was used to losing things precious to her. It didn't make it any easier.

A week later she was sitting in her kitchen trying to come to terms with a feeling that was gnawing at her. It was, after all, part of the profession. She had been far more susceptible in her youth and never had waited for a missed period to alert her. It had been a daily thing, checking her breasts for swelling, nipples sore, signs of sickness, not wanting her coffee in the morning. That was usually the one. If the smell of the coffee pot ever turned up her nose she went straight for the remedy cupboard. First were the old wives solutions, vile potions to drink, stinking baths to sit in, but for the most part they worked. Then there were things she could do herself. It was rare for her to have to take a trip into the town for a real doctor to put paid to one of Mother Nature's little efforts. It had happened though. And the one time she felt sure it was the Gardener's she had left it be. That would have been nice, she reflected. The child would be about Joseph's age now. A stupid lump gathered in her throat from out of nowhere but she managed to swallow it away with the thought that God knew best and she would abide by his decision as always. She had gone to her sister's in Virginia, never telling a soul, not even the Gardener. She had no thoughts on how it might turn out; would she give up her work and care for it? Leave the child in Virginia and send money? First she had to see the child, to find out how she would feel. Only then would she be able to decide.

But God saved her the trouble and took back the little soul before it could make a start. But he made her labor for it first. And Sally had made the nurse show it to her though it was hardly bigger than some she had aborted herself. Four months too early little fella, she told him again now, out loud. She often talked to her dead son. Impetuous was nothing you ever inherited from me, she said.

God had known, of course. God saved the little soul and took it back to try again. Next time it might manage both arms and two little feet ... and a proper family to raise it, she thought.

Sally looked again at the cold pot of yesterday's coffee she had brought as far as the sink and knew she wouldn't be cleaning it out for a fresh brew after all. Could it be? Already? It was little more than a week. She slipped back the lapels of her wrapper, shaking them free over her shoulders, leaving her breasts naked in the cool of the morning kitchen air. With her right hand she brushed the hardness of her left nipple and felt its difference. Not larger, smaller, harder, hotter ...none of those things. Just different.

She felt it was Joe's, too. There was no question, she declared, it was just one of those things you felt you knew. What she wasn't sure was what to do next.

She set the coffee pot on the side and went over to settle herself in the rocker. It was then Mr Clarkson's car sounded in the track behind the house and she knew he would be at the porch just as soon as she turned around. He was the very last person on earth she wanted visiting. He was the one customer she could do without today.

She pulled her wrapper more modestly round her and tied the belt tight over her stomach. She would just have to tell him it was not convenient right now. At the back of her mind she wondered if it might ever be convenient again. For him or anyone.

Chapter 5

With a stick, Old Loula slowly drew her name in the dust at her feet. The man watched her. It took a long time and the concentration was written on Old Loula's face.

So the story comes a circle back to us three women at the spigot, she continued. Larded and bunioned Libby, long lean Sissie Jane and me, Loula, they all saw as a old grump. As I recollect it was just about then Libby got pressed into spelling out the letters for young Hester in the dust by the spigot. Of course we didn't know what Hester had in mind at first, and why she thought book reading would help her with history and the voices in her head, but Libby went along with it and was showing off as far as I could see. Libby and me didn't always see eye-to-eye them days.

Most of the letters Libby was sure of, but there was one or two as foxed her memory a touch, and Libby never was one to show a failing of any kind. It can squarely be said that of the 26 letters she only forgot the K, a useless consonant that had nothing to offer above and beyond that of a C anyhow, or so she said when finally reminded of her omission. Also, it was several years into real book learning before Hester could rid herself finally of Libby's belief that the tail of a Y swept over toward the right. And it was a long time before Q came into focus, was the polite way Hester put it. I recall the powerful look coming over Libby's face every time she tried to mark out a small Q, for I chose never to let on but I was working as hard as Hester at learning my alphabet those days out by the spigot. I can just about read these days but I won't mention it, least of all to Libby. Anyroad, Libby's attempts at teaching a small Q always ended with it looking far too much like the small G and she would scratch it out then scratch her head, then try writing a Q and a G together until she could no longer figure out the either of them, as she would say. Her final cure was to use capitals for both regardless of where they fell in the word and this was how Hester learned to spell.

Hester did her lessons with a stick, her best chalkboard being the dampened dust where she would take the long side of a orange crate box and drag its edge over the lessons of the day before to make herself a clean slate of red mud. There she would set herself down and write out her name and as many of the lessons as Libby could recall from her own young days at the big house, with the red shoes. That story of the red shoes was precious to Libby and she would tell it over and over to any folk she could get to set and listen long enough.

The day she got the red shoes was the day Libby knew she was going places. Her mother traveled north and got herself a job as live-in maid at some big house just in Harlem and then sent for Libby to join her. Well, maybe it was a bit further out than Harlem itself but it was still the biggest place Libby had ever seen. Their room out the back was plenty big enough for herself, her mother and the man she was to call 'uncle'. He was okay, she said, and he did buy her the shoes after all. The red shoes meant she could dance at the Palais even though she was only thirteen. And could she dance.

Everything changed just around then. Not just her and the shoes but the whole damn world. Suddenly black was interesting to folks in the north. Ragtime thumped from the most fashionable of white quarters ... but only from the most fashionable mind, it was still unforgivable bad taste for all southerners and those with old money. For the young in Harlem the blues was something to smile about. Gentlefolk paid good money to hear black men sing and watch black girls dance. And to watch their long black adolescent legs flashing quick to the quick steps and see their skirts whirling high, more like. If you was dancing you had to smile and say it was fun and show sex oozing from your big black lips. But not too big. Libby was about right for a white audience. Her butt was tight still and her bust high, her face just brown enough to be naughty but light enough for white folks to find attractive. And her lips pouty but not so big as to offend.

What the white folks did not know was the only real fun to be had was back in the black quarter where there was no fancy clubs and no white folks. The rent parties was held in people's houses and apartments and they rattled the buildings and the streets clear into the morning. If a man wanted to raise money to pay his rent, he just gathered round his musician friends, set up the drink and charged admission. There was always good rent parties going on most nights of the week.

Even the folks at the big house, where her mother worked and Libby now lived-in, even they joined in the new Harlem fashion and took to considering that black people might be human after all ... the talented one's that is. The daughter Susan was instructed to have Libby join her in the yard after her schoolwork was done so they could discuss music and culture together. Black poets were getting in print just then and Susan would read some passages to Libby in the evenings she wasn't working at the Palais. She also got her early readers out the attic and let Libby work through the exercises.

Those were the days of the red shoes. The days of the National Association for the Advancement of Colored People. The days when life tricked Libby into believing she might just be important. But the depression stole in like a black cloud and the whites closed ranks like the NAACP never happened. Jobs was too scarce for whites to share with blacks, and it turned out ideals is just a luxury after all. Libby's chest started busting out of that satin top at about the same time as her ass turned too animal for a fashion as thought a woman should have no shape at all. Her feet grew two sizes, almost splitting the red shoes clear off their soles, just as the 20's bubble burst. She was sent back to the South where she was raised, clutching the precious shoes in a brown carrier.

But Libby had picked up the basics in life, including some book learning, and she passed on what she knew to Hester.

By then Libby would kick off her dusty brown no-good loafers, all stretched out with bunion swellings and looking for all the world like two red yams, and scratch at the insole of her foot with the other big toe just at the thought of book learning. And when she looked down and her misshapen big toes surprised her, as they always did the way they lay diagonal like that, her feet going straight up and then taking a turn at the bunions and charging off left and right, when she saw that, she thought each time of those days in her youth when she believed she was going someplace.

So Libby taught and Hester learned and I listened until we knew everything that one old lady at a spigot can remember, plus a lot of things she thought she half remembered and a few that pride allowed her to invent.

There was more involved than just the knowledge of reading. All in all it took Hester two years to ready herself for the big trip into town. This wasn't no trek to the store with her daddy to deliver Mr Clarkson's car, for it was Solomon now as did the engine fixing and of the few folks that noted any connection between the Clarkson's and Joe's death none was willing to say. Nor was the journey a mere collecting of a sack of flour in a neighbor's truck. This took two years of preparation because Hester was going to the library. And there was a libary too, right in the next big town just west of here, and a school, a black one where the black and colored kids could go if their folks wasn't hicks and lived too far out and didn't have the time for learning anyhow on account of the work needing to be done in the fields. So there was black schooling and black facilities, Hester knew that, but until now they had not been on offer to her. She was too proud to walk into the library until she was confident they weren't about to throw her right out again.

* * *

And there was one other Hester confided in during those two years of learning and that was Sally, the forbidden woman down by the crick. Two others really, on account of her son Little Joseph being a very ready and willing ear for anything she cared to tell him. He learned all about the pink map and the strange girl with one arm and one leg not right. Before he was a year old he knew more of Hester's story than anyone. And he was a beautiful baby. Strong and plump with a smile always on his face and one fist jammed in his mouth to rub his sore gums with. He was just like a cherub, chubby legged and smiling like any painting and the dribble glistening on his chin the only thing needed to embellish the picture. Not that I ever pretended to notice at the time for Sally was a outcast to us back then, but you couldn't help but watch the treasure of a child growing up, he was that precious. He reminded me a lot of Joe.

'Hi Little Joseph,' Hester would say, arriving on the porch and bending down to pat the tight wool on his head.

Sally never heard the half of it from Hester herself but she caught more than was intended through open windows and doors on the latch. Sally never criticized other folks for being strange; I'll give her that.

* * *

Finally, Hester was ten years old.

Sissie Jane got the ride arranged for Hester and her friend Mary Ellen, who was set to meet her mother at a park near where she worked, and the two of them girls worked all that week to plait their hair and mend and wash their very best dresses. Hester all but boiled the print off hers was what I told her, as she set to getting it clean enough for the occasion, but Sissie did her usual look at me from down her nose like I know nothing, so then I shut up which is what she meant for me to do. Sissie always accuses me of being a sour old grump but she can be mean spirited herself, I can tell you. I don't know where I get this reputation for always saying the wrong thing but you ask any folk round these parts and that is what they tell you.

Anyroad, I'm getting away from the point. Now if they was to accuse me of wandering off the point then that would be valid, because I do that a great deal and I will admit to it, but a moaner I am not. Where was I? Yes, Hester, she had near plagued us with questions before this library day dawned. It wasn't enough just to teach her reading and point her in the direction of the library; she told us she needed some idea of the protocol before she could go in. She wanted to know from Libby just what happened behind those big carved wood doors she knew she would find. How could she look at the books? Who could she ask? Was she allowed? Was it the same here as in the big cities where Libby had been book reading? None of us could be specific about the answers although one of Libby's daughter's lived near the town and she had bragged about how coloreds could definitely use the library.

When Hester had smartened herself to the best she knew how, face scrubbed and shining, the dust washed from her shoes and them both buffed up with a cloth with all the elbow grease Libby could muster, Hester was ready for her ride to the town. Even I had dug out a hat for her. It was a serious occasion, I recognized that, and Hester would not let Mary Ellen reduce it by her giggling. Sissie Jane said it was the sight of Hester in my felt hat as started her laughing but Hester put that down to Mary Ellen not having seen her mother for some time and her being nervous of the event.

Finally they got into the truck and set off to the town. When they arrived the truck pulled up outside the municipal building and Hester was let out the back. If I know Hester and her pride she would of pulled

that felt hat of mine more firmly onto her head and made herself walk
tall before crossing the square.

Chapter 6

Old Loula sat forward and picked up a handful of small stones that she pitched at the side of her pail. She didn't speak for quite a while and the man wondered if she remembered he was there.

Now, where was I, she asked herself eventually. It seemed that Old Loula dropped a stitch but, despite what folk said, she had the patience to draw it back up. Yes, she said, I recall now, it was that day at the library.

The library doors was just as Hester had imagined them, she said, high at the top of a flight of stone steps. She stood in the street and looked at the polished wood all cool in the hot sun. One of the double doors was just ajar and the deep shadows inside promised her everything. She was in no hurry to go inside. It had been a long journey to get this far, she told herself, there was no need to rush. Besides, she was scared just a touch.

A boy went by on a bicycle and all but mowed her down. Dust clouded up from his wheels and she had to brush at her dress.

'Hey,' shouted the boy 'what's that possum critter sat on your head?'

Hester wanted to shout the rude words she had heard Joe cursing under his breath, but the boy was bigger than she was, twelve or thirteen maybe, and she decided against spoiling her best ever day for some two-bit skunk of a no-nothing low-life. Instead she took off the hat and folded it tight into a handful of felt so it could of been any object she might be carrying. Then she crossed all the way over the wide square and set off up the library steps. At last she was getting near to finding the books that might explain the life inside her head. She was looking for history.

Hester never saw the sign, or if she saw something on the wall then she paid it no mind and certainly never stopped to piece the letters together into words that would tell her that vital piece of information. The only word she saw was the one she was looking for; LIBRARY was chiseled large and white above the doors.

It was only when the stern looking white woman behind the desk let out a scream that everyone turned to look at Hester. Then a tall man in a dark suit and a gray hat strode big strides over to where she had stopped just inside the door and all but picked her up by the shoulder in his hurry to get her back out into the street. She would have gone anyhow. One look at that screaming woman's face and Hester was set to turn and run if only her legs would do as they was asked. She was in the wrong place, the woman's face told her that. And the sign on the outside wall, that the tall, hatted man was pointing her at now, spelled it out, WHITES ONLY. NO COLORED.

Libby's daughter was right in part. There was a library for colored folk, so long as they didn't mind it being a windowless basement room round behind, under the library fire exit steps. Maybe it wasn't so bad if you found it straight off and weren't stinging from embarrassment but all Hester could see was a dingy room scantily shelved with tired books cast off from upstairs. The one bare bulb hung in the center of the room so the shadows fell round the shelved walls and left a pool of gloom around the desk on the far side. It was the librarian's desk and she was peering into the pages of a book she held angled away from her, trying to catch the best of the light. Hester was consoled by her black face and the small nod she gave in acknowledgment.

That first visit to the library was a failure. The lump in Hester's throat was now so big she couldn't swallow past it and her eyes were hot and ready to cry. She just stared at the rows of books. Stared and stared herself into a trance so she never heard when the librarian looked up and spoke.

'You need any help honey?'

The accent was from the north, clipped and quick, not like the slower speak of these parts. But it was not unfriendly.

'I said, you need help honey, you just give me a call. All right?'

The librarian got up from her desk and walked over to where Hester was standing, though she could still see precious little because Hester was facing the books and was stood so close to the shelves. All she could see was that the girl had stopped moving, as if she was asleep or something.

'You okay?' the librarian asked.

The librarian had seen her own brother sleepwalking and it was the same kind of thing except this girl was most definitely awake a moment ago. The minutes ticked by and she thought maybe she should call a doctor. Then she wondered who would thank her when it came to paying the bill. Best to wait a while and see.

The librarian had been right up close to the child's face, looking for signs of some sense in her, but now she went back to her desk on the far side of the room and bided her time, turning her pencil round and round in her fingers. She tapped it loudly on the desk a few times, to see if the noise would register any movement in the girl, but it seemed she didn't notice. Patiently, she picked up her book from the desk and found her place on the page, then she started to read. Mainly because she could think of nothing else to do.

After a few minutes the child shook her head and the very spirit of her seemed to come back.

'The Lord have mercy,' said the librarian softly to herself.

The tears gushed quickly now down Hester's face and she started to shake in an embarrassed panic.

'You need help there?' asked the librarian, to help her out. Then she put down her own book and walked over once more.

Hester shook her head because she didn't trust her voice not to come out with a squeak. As far as Hester knew, she had just entered the room from the library upstairs and she was still smarting from the white lady's screams. Unless things changed around her she often didn't know about her times of petit mal. Turning away quickly she pretended to be reading the book titles, but the words on the spines blurred through the tears. She brushed her eyes dry with the crumpled ball of felt hat she still held in her hand and then pulled out a book, any book and opened the pages. The letters were so small and so close, so different to her words formed in the mud and dust at the spigot. She looked at the printed shapes through the tears, willing them to change into words she recognized but they just stayed as marks on the page. Hester was afraid and her two fears joined forces against her. The first fear, the horror of trespassing her black feet on the white library floor, stung at her pride, telling her she was foolish. She had, after all, missed the fundamental words, the ones now branded on her soul, the letters never spelled out by her or Libby on the dust, NO COLORED. The other fear was for the pink areas on the map that were her only clues to the search she had set herself. Fear that she may not find the place; fear that she might. Hester was frightened of the years piling up in front of her while she searched, and this jumbled itself with the fear of finding and unlocking the unknown.

The gentle voice of the librarian cut through Hester's thoughts.

'Here,' said the woman, 'this is the best light for reading,' and she moved a chair into the center of the room just under the light bulb.

Hester always knew what she wanted but now she felt she would never find it here. The right book would tell her everything, show her the damp mists swirling at her feet, remind her of the life in her head. The librarian had asked if she would like some help. The answer was yes, yes, she needed someone to tell her where the book was. It would be part of a pink map. In fact, she thought it had a lot to do with pink. Could she have betrayed everything she knew and been pink herself? No ... there was no reason to burn pink, only black, and it had to do with burning, she thought that too. Or was it more linked to the water? It was the map that would be pink, great swathes of pink, page after page, and there she would find herself, poppy pink. Were poppies pink? No, she thought they were red but she wasn't sure. They didn't grow round these parts.

The librarian asked again did she want help and Hester put back the book she had open in her hands and said no. She couldn't do it after all. Then she ran quickly across the room, flew outside into the daylight and decided to wait for the ride home. It would be hours yet but she didn't mind sitting on a railing in the sun, kicking her feet in the dust. The only thing she minded was not having the book. Not having any book. She had nothing to show for her two years of learning from Libby. Now she had let Libby down as well as herself.

The boy on the bicycle rode past again and she quickly stuffed the felt hat under her dress before he could see it.

'I could'a told you that was the wrong libary,' he bragged and Hester felt smoke must be rising from her cheeks they were so hot. 'Can't you read?' he said.

The boy, had she known it, was Libby's 4th grandchild for it was Libby's daughter who lived in the town and had told them of the library.

'Yes sir I certainly can read,' said Hester 'and I will be getting myself a book in just one minute after I have taken the air. It was a mite stuffy in there with all them books for company.'

With that she raised her chin about as high as it would go while still attached to her neck and slipped off the railing. The hat fell in the dirt. She had a mind to leave it there but she thought she would be skinned alive for losing it so she had to bend and pick it up. She wished she had enough sass to brush it off there and then in front of him, deliberately, but she couldn't rise to it. It was going to take all her effort just to get back in the library room.

That was how she ended up with the blue book on engineering and it took most of the journey back in the truck for her to decipher the title. Hester walked back into the room and chose a book with a blue cover before her eyes had even adjusted to the light, but the librarian lady never made her feel stupid like the boy on the bicycle had done.

'I am wanting to join the libary,' she said bravely, placing the book on the desk. 'If that's all right,' she added in a much smaller voice.

'It is most certainly all right young lady,' said the librarian. 'And you are sure this is the book you want?' The woman turned the book so she could read the title.

Hester could feel the lump growing in her throat again. It was all going wrong. She was too young to take this book. The woman wouldn't give it to her. She would have to leave empty handed and the boy would be outside laughing at her, she knew he would be.

'This book?' the librarian repeated.

Hester looked at the door, weighing up the boy against the librarian.

'You can have this book if you want it,' said the woman. 'Would you like me to write you out a ticket?'

A ticket? Yes, that was what she needed. Libby had said about a library ticket. She would need a ticket. She nodded her head, yes, and the woman stamped the inside of the book and said she might sit on the chair, the one under the light in the middle of the room, while she completed the ticket and would she come back over in a minute to spell out her name and say where she lived? Hester nodded and bobbed a strange curtsey that even she herself thought was a little odd, before taking the blue book to the chair where she puzzled over the first page.

A short time later she carried the book, recorded under her own ticket and date stamped, proudly out of the library room and across the street but the boy on the bicycle had gone. The railings didn't seem quite the right seating arrangement for such a grand book as this so Hester took a walk to the crossroads and sat herself down, taking care to keep the blue cover free from dust. She refused to let herself cry despite the thoughts that kept coming, repeating in her head the incidents of the day, interrupting her as she tried so hard to decipher the printed letters, stopping her mind from making words and sounds. The book wasn't right, said a small voice in her head; it wasn't the one she wanted; there were no pink maps, no water ... no explanation of the other person inside of her. Then suddenly she started to cry. She cried for herself and for the girl in the water. The water rising. Did the water rise or the girl sink? Hester could feel the cold water around her ankles and the mud slink between her toes. The mud was warmer but it sucked at her, making it difficult to keep walking, walking, heavier on one side than the other, further into the water, the water getting higher around her, pulling her dress down so it caught between her legs, her thighs. Then her dress floated up, free, buoyed her almost, and it was impossible to walk for her feet were no longer on the ground. It was the others beside her, holding her hands, that kept her moving forwards, deeper, further, keeping the panic out of her heart with their chanting. What was the song? She almost had it on her tongue. The words ... her hair floating up beside her in the water ... and the bubbles in the water, the water warm now except for the shivering inside of her, the bubbles coming out from her own mouth as she repeated the words Helly had taught her ... Isis, Istase ...

And then it was gone. She was back at the crossroads and a car was blowing its horn as it overtook an old station wagon. The dust flew up in a tornado and choked her for a minute but she wouldn't let go of the thoughts. Isis. That was the only word she could grasp. She got a stick and wrote it in the dust just to plant it firmly in her head. Isis. It was satisfying. It was a start.

* * *

The librarian's name was Abigail and after Hester was gone she started sorting through a large box of books passed on from upstairs. Abigail had religion. Not the loud magnificent kind like Sissie Jane, where God is openly appealed to on every occasion where his judgment might prove Sissie to be right and her adversary to be transgressing. No, this was a quiet belief that gave Abigail strength even in her most tired moments. Like now. If others would only go home at night and consult the good book, as she did, then they might see the error of their ways and maybe together they could start piecing this country into a righteous place to live.

Abigail had come south from New York with some high ideals when she was younger and stronger, but now she was older and quite worn out with it all. And for two pins she would have left the strange girl in the library to sort herself out, if the truth were known, because she'd just about had a bellyful of dealing with the overflow books from the town library. She never would call it the white library. That was the bottom line. She never would call it that. Books were books and they knew no color of their own. It was the withholding of books and education that was a color problem and libraries, she knew, were intended for distribution of language. That was what she had believed in the beginning. The Lord only knew what she believed now and he seemed to have no plans for letting Abigail in on the secret. Her fighting days were just about finished.

Anyway, it wasn't the overflow of books that was the problem, it was Mr Big arranging for them to be brought down in their boxes and coming down himself to supervise. His insistence that they were newer books than those on the shelves, therefore she should dispose of the same quantity to make room, did not strike her with the same element of logic that it did him. She made the point that if only he would release some more bookshelves or let her have overflow free-standing ones ... and she knew there were some lying idle in his stockroom because she had seen them ... she had plenty of floor space to accommodate both old and new books. She tried to show him that some of his latest cast-offs were less use to her than the existing books and she would not throw out good research material or basic educational tools to make room for lame white trashy novels with no relevance, although she had omitted the word white. And who was the librarian in charge downstairs anyway, she had asked him? She always phrased it 'downstairs' as if it was geographical, just one more category, 'fiction ground floor, reference on mezzanine and decent folk downstairs'.

It had been a difficult day and she would go home from her work that night to settle on a quiet chair with just her and God and the good book to check she had not transgressed any of his laws in trying to defend the education of her town yet again. Sometimes she wondered from the thin trickle of visitors if her work was of any use to anyone. The only thing she did know for certain was that the downstairs library would never have existed in the first place without her efforts and her appeals to the state government to step in and spell out the law of America to the local judge.

Despite her weariness and the boxes of books she was sorting through, there was something about that skinny girl today that woke her up. She wished she had done more now. She should have given the girl a reader. She knew it at the time and she knew it more now, but Abigail was also cautious not to scare the child. It took guts to come in a library when you couldn't read. You had to take your hat off to the girl. And it was important that Abigail move slowly if she was to be a lasting help, she knew that. She smiled to herself as she realized with pleasure that it was children like that frightened girl she had come here for, leaving her folks and her chance of marriage in New York, not to sour the morning arguing with Mr Big from the mezzanine floor. Yet it was easy to forget. She must be more alert next time. And she must watch out for the girl's next visit.

'What was her name?' Abigail asked herself aloud, pulling the wooden slide drawer towards her with the pitifully few library tickets all logged neatly in date order for the book returns in three weeks. She found it. 'Hester P Jefferson,' she said quietly. 'Well Miss H P Jefferson, I surely hope you will come back and visit your downstairs library again real soon.'

Chapter 7

Old Loula felt the heat on the back of her neck and knew a drink of cool water would help. She let a stream of water run from the spigot and cupped some in her hand. The well-dressed man took the opportunity to pull a small notebook from his leather case and wrote down a few notes. When Old Loula had drunk she turned to shoo a chicken away from the bench and then took her place again. Before speaking she looked up at the sun and told the man she could spare just another hour.

I recall that evening with a smile these days, she went on, that evening after Hester's first visit to the library. We was sitting at the spigot as always and Libby tried to make light of the engineering book saying as how it would be best to start with something a mite complex on account of everything that followed would be a piece of cake. It certainly was a challenge to Libby, I can say, for it must of been many years since she herself had seen a book of any kind. It impressed Sissie Jane that Libby could explain any of the printed words at all, but I thought it best to say nothing. Eventually Hester and Libby made some headway and before long it was time to return the book.

The second trip to the library seemed to go a lot better for Hester, or so she said, what with her confidence being higher this time, and she spent two hours searching before she found what she was looking for, opening book after book until she found it. Then suddenly it was there, in her hands, the large patches of pink that had haunted her dreams. She had found a atlas.

The librarian had a surprise for her too.

'I've been expecting you,' she said when Hester went to check out her treasure, the atlas. She was given a second ticket and a reader. Abigail explained how the reader would help with her book learning and that when she had done with Reader Stage One, there were six more to follow.

'More books on engines? I asked Hester when she got back.

'Eng'neering,' corrected Libby. I was joking of course, but it got taken the wrong way as usual.

'Leave the child be,' said Sissie Jane, bossing us around as she always did and treating me and Libby like two children ourselves.

Hester had run straight up from where the truck had dropped her at the turning and she stooped breathless for a moment, looking at us three women sitting by the spigot, the reader and the precious atlas enormous in her skinny arms.

'It's here,' she gasped at last. 'The pink. I found it.'

She sat down a few feet away and opened the atlas on her knees, carefully turning the pages and passing the pink areas on all the maps until she came to a page with one pink island the shape of a hunched old man, a small parcel in the crook of a larger land. Us three women just looked at each other and said nothing.

'Here,' she said, her fingers tracing the words. 'Greet ... brit .. ayne.'

Hester looked up and saw we was puzzled.

'So?' I asked her, waiting to be enlightened.

At that point she had never told us what we was to learn later. All those times she nearly confided in Sissie but she never had known where to start; with the girl in her head or with the burning flesh and sweet magnolias? Then it was too late. How could she start in the middle with us three looking at her like that? With the pink map open on her knees and her just finding the place after all this time? She wriggled in front of us, wanting our help yet not knowing how to explain it all when none of it was explainable. Sissie Jane stood up and walked the few steps over to Hester's side.

'Tell us about the map Hester,' she said kindly.

Hester's mouth opened but no words came out. There was no place to start.

'You been there before?' asked Sissie with that soft voice like she was ready to understand any crazy thing. Her eyes sucked Hester out, wanting her to say something. A couple moments went by then Sissie moved in real close and hunkered down, her lean shadow falling on the book and her large dry skinned bony hand hovering over the page.

'Tell me where you was, child. Point it out for me,' she said. 'It was on the pink piece, right?'

Hester nodded yes.

'Show me e'sakly,' said Sissie Jane.

Hester placed her hand squarely on the page and her finger all but covered the small island.

'Let me have a look see,' said Libby 'I seen a atlas before.' She squatted on the ground on the other side of Hester and extended a rounded arm over the child's thin shoulder. 'That there is England, see? And Great Britain is the name if you add on all the other bits that I don't rightly recall the names of just now. And here,' she moved a finger to the right and picked out the names 'you have France and Germany ... and there is Spain look.'

I wandered over too but pretended not to pay much mind. Sissie would only scold me for poking my nose in so it was best not to seem interested.

'England,' repeated Hester slowly. 'I didn't know it was England. I just knew I would find it.'

'And way on this side,' Libby was showing off now, 'this here big piece is Russia.'

'Is it shown anyplace bigger?' Sissie Jane asked of Libby, meaning the scale of the map.

'Surely. Let me take a look here.' Libby flipped backwards and forwards through the large pages until she found the south of England alone, spread across two pages. Hester's eyes were on stalks at the sight of it.

'Do you know what we are looking for?' asked Sissie.

Hester pointed to the east coastline, about a third of the way up.

'Ipswich ' Libby read.

'No. Not that,' Hester insisted.

I made a point of taking a deep sigh and went back to the wood bench.

'Colchester?' read Libby.

'No.'

'Well that's right under your finger,' Libby said.

Sissie Jane gave her a small prod and Libby read out the names of other places on the page. 'Wivenhoe, Clacton, Walton-on-the-Naze, Brightlingsea ... '

Hester inclined her head a little.

'... West Mersea ...' continued Libby.

'Mersea?' repeated Hester, no longer looking at the book on her knees but gazing way off into the sky, past where I sat patiently scooping the flies from my water pail. 'Mersea Island on the Blackwater River ...' she said.

Libby checked. 'Sure thing. It's on the River Blackwater.'

'But you're too far to the south Libby, you're down in the mud flats,' said Hester. 'Much further south and you'll be into dangerous water. Try the names higher.'

Libby's knees were giving out so she hitched her dress up some and sat down beside Hester, stretching her legs out in front and kicking her feet free of her shoes. The bunions was normally objects of great fascination for Hester but this time she never noticed. Libby looked closer and read out more names. 'Wrabness, Parkestop, Harwich ...'

'Upriver from Harwich,' said Hester.

'New Mistley ...' continued Libby.

'Not New Mistley,' Hester jumped in, 'Mistley Thorn. And Manningtree.'

Yes, Manningtree's here,' said Libby 'but I don't see no Mistley Thorn.'

'But it must be there,' implored Hester, 'Mistley Thorn ... the Thorn Inn at Mistley ... facing the estuary ... and there's a round pond in front of it.

Libby was scratching at her head and I was pitching stones at the hens by then, but Sissie Jane didn't seem surprised.

'Manningtree rogues and Mistley malcontents,' Hester said to herself.

'Well I don't see no Mistley Thorn here but there is Manningtree train station ...' said Libby.

'Don't be silly Libby,' said Hester 'why would there be a station? There are no trains yet.'

Sissie Jane and Libby just looked at each other after that.

*   *   *

As Hester told me later, that day was the most perfect she ever dream possible. The four of us sat by the spigot and exploring the atlas until Hester had all but told us near everything, about the strange pale girl so far away in another time with the weak arm and leg, but she didn't tell us then about Joe. How could she say she knew all along he would be burnt without it sounding like she could of saved him. Why didn't you tell us Hester, we would of said? Yet she had known it so many years, how could we have protected him? No, she had to bear that part of the secret by herself for it was too terrible to tell.

Hester, Libby and Sissie Jane all poured over the atlas until it was too dark to make out anything more. Even I went over to look a couple of times. Then we all went back to our homes, with Sissie Jane taking the book for safekeeping because Solomon never did seem to understand the importance of such things.

And it was then, on that precious day, that Hester's father touched her. First he beat her, for going to the library or reading or some such excuse. Even he wasn't too clear on the reason it seemed. Maybe it was on account of there being no supper ready but Sissie Jane had cleared that in advance because of the library visit. It was the beating that raised the spirit in him, sending Hester sprawling across the floor on her back and reminding him of her mother. Or so folks said. Maybe she just reminded him of a women's body on its back. Her body was too young to know but her mind had a good idea that something had changed between them. He touched places that she knew was wrong. But the blows never knocked the sense into her that Solomon intended and she vowed to go back to the library just as soon as the bruising went down. But there was a place to visit in the meantime, for all she would never tell Sissie Jane of it for shame. She would be off to see Miss Sally and the baby just as soon as she could, knowing there would be a welcome for her, bruises and all.

* * *

That next evening Solomon was sitting in his chair, looking all set to take a smoke of his pipe. First he cleaned it out and tapped it against the table the way he always did, then he reached for the tobacco with smooth, clean fingers. There was no grease on them tonight for all he had Mr Clarkson's piston rings out that afternoon. His hands was scrubbed clean, scrubbed almost to blisters with the lye soap and still no cleaner for it, in his own mind. Solomon looked over at the bar of yellow soap still wet against the washboard and then his own hands stung at his eyes when he went to brush off the tears there. It must of been that the dried off soap still had some power. He rubbed the tobacco over his hands, as anxious now to be rid of the soap as he had been to wash off the guilt before. When he smelled his hands again they were a little better but not much. They smelled of tobacco and lye and her and hisself. He'd smelled it all day, working on them pistons, washing off all them parts in gasoline trying to hide it.

Solomon leaned back in the chair and closed his eyes. He was tired from not having slept the night before. He'd just gone outside and walked all round till the light was coming up at last. He'd been afraid to close his eyes because he would see his own shame there, that was how he reckoned. He figured all the while he could feed in pictures from the outside world then his mind could latch on to something else. If he closed that off he would be faced with what he had done.

His eyes were hot but they itched worse with them closed, so he sat up and finished with filling his pipe. He unlaced and kicked off his boots before striking a match and inhaling the smoke. The first pull relaxed him but the aftertaste was of lye soap.

'Damn,' he swore and spat out onto the floor.

'But I only touched her Lord,' he said, trying to reassure himself and his maker that it could have been worse. 'I would never do more than that. I wouldn't do the other thing. That would be real bad with your own daughter.'

Now the thought of what he hadn't completed stirred him again as he pictured Hester's legs. He gripped the stem of the pipe so hard it broke in two.

'Never,' he said aloud to himself. 'I won't never touch her again.'

And he thought he meant it.

'Lord help me 'cause I don't deserve to live on this here earth if I lays one finger on that girl again. Lord, if I lie you just feel free to take me any time you decide. It'd be right nice to see my wife anyways.'

He wept then. He recalled fetching Sissie Jane to the cabin that night when his wife was in labor and pints of her lifeblood pouring out of her as he watched. He remembered his wife mumbling. Solomon had puzzled it many times over the years and was sure she had been talking sense if only he had been able to understand her. It wasn't like she was ranting, Solomon had seen drunks ranting, this was different, like she was talking direct to someone, but it was not to him. "Don't let them burn her ... tell her to take my hand into the water ... rather the water than the flames ... we choose the water". He thought of her face bleached out on the bed like that to a dry yellow and the linen-white turning redder with every moment until he could do nothing but leave little Joey under the table where he hid from the screams and start running for Sissie. He knew as he ran that his wife would die. There was only so much blood in a body and most of hers was puddling into the mattress.

Sweet Jesus, he thought now, no way could that woman and I meet in the same place after what tempted me last night. God wrote the rule book and it was quite plain to see, even for a man as never read it hisself. Maybe God was not kind enough to punish him, he started to think, maybe God made it harder than that. Would he be obliged to deliver up hisself? He shivered, put down the broken pipe and went out to walk yet again.

*   *   *

Hester went over to bide time with the forbidden Miss Sally, and Sally was glad of the company, what with her not allowing the men round to visit, and her an outcast from other folk as always. There was few now as bothered to call on Sally except the bald gardener and a few children who threw stones at her windows as they chanted bad words about her son having no father. Not that Sally minded the insults. Yet she was that proud of her strong son she wondered how others felt they could blame him for his own parents. Things seemed so clear cut to her, there was times she just wanted to explain good sense to others. It seemed many of them never had any of their own. She wished sometimes she had been a school teacher.

Little Joseph was playing on the floor when Sally showed Hester into the kitchen.

Sally noticed something wrong straight off. It wasn't just the bruise swelling under Hester's eye; it was the sadness in all her face. As sad as when they burned her brother. Sally just hoped her life's work had saved a few Hesters along the way. There had been many times she had worked for free rather than send troubled men back to their daughters.

Sally did what she would continue to do for Hester, she gave her time and quietness, never forcing conversation to fill the silences but allowing the girl to sit playing with Joseph if that was what she needed.

Hester became a frequent visitor and often read her books out loud to Joseph who sometimes listened and other times tottered placidly round where she sat on the green rug on the floor. Hester would let herself in after a light knock on the porch screen door and often as not Sally would not know of the visitor until she heard, through an open window or door, a thin voice asking a question of Joseph. Little Joseph's vocabulary was limited but he often gurgled back a gibberish response that seemed to serve its purpose and allow Hester to move forward in her thinking.

Hester worked through the readers with Abigail, the librarian, and gradually written words on the page started to make some sense, but it now seemed she would exhaust the books in the downstairs library before finding any more clues to the past she remembered. Eventually Abigail found them a first link in the chain.

'Here it is,' shouted Abigail from the other side of the library room. She looked at the printed sign on her own desk. Silence, it said. 'I knew it. Seek and ye shall find,' she finished in a loud whisper.

Abigail took the book to where the bulb hung in the center of the room, under which she had taken to placing a small card table together with a chair. It was Hester's special reading place; she spent so much time in the library these days. Many times she would get into town and not be sure of a ride home, but there was always Libby's daughter who would find her a place to sleep with her own children. That's where she found the boy on the bicycle who had taunted her the first trip to the library. His name was Jesse and he was three years older than Hester. He never had stopped teasing her and it seemed she would never stop being embarrassed.

'I knew it would be here someplace,' said Abigail as she studied the words under her fingers. 'Chapter 12, History of pre-Christian England. Osiris, Isis and Horus, a trinity based on an ancient Egyptian triad.'

Isis, thought Hester, remembering the word she had written in the dust that afternoon of her first visit to the library. Isis. It had meant something to her or to the person inside her but she did not know what and it was the only word she could remember, the link that made her feel the water again, the mud between her toes and then her body floating up ... and then down. Hester shivered.

'Who is she?' Hester wanted to know.

'How did you know it was a woman?' asked Abigail.

'It just felt like a woman's name.'

'Not many folk I've found called Isis,' said Abigail. She looked down on the page but there was only one more mention, '... and as Christianity was adopted throughout England, often against the will of the population, the trinity of Osiris, Isis and Horus were replaced by the holy figures of God, Mary and Jesus.'

'What about God the Father, the Son and the Holy Ghost?' asked Hester.

'It doesn't say.'

'Did they take Mary out of the trinity because she was a woman?' asked Hester who was catching on.

'You, young lady,' said Abigail, 'may turn out to be just too smart for your own good.'

She looked down at Hester's wide set eyes. Abigail went back to the book, tracing the line of fine print with her finger as she read, to make sure she didn't miss a word of their first clue in Hester's search. Abigail's beliefs couldn't find a happy place for the idea of reincarnation so she never allowed that idea to grow as such. What she did believe was the child's honesty. If Hester knew of pink atlases, of drowning and of ancient names, Abigail didn't mind if it was remembered or seen before it happened. The child had a gift of sight and who was to specify the difference in hearing voices from the past and from God? They burned dear Saint Joan for her voices and that was a grievous error of human judgment as far as Abigail was concerned.

'It says here,' continued Abigail, 'that the old religion went back over 25,000 years and was led primarily by women priests.' Abigail brushed a hand through her hair as if to catch a loose strand but it was just to give her fingers something to do. 'The old gods who were worshipped combined both good and bad qualities,' she went on, 'expressing whims, temper and generosity. It was only with the advent of Christianity and the God of love that sin was born. The new God was so good that all bad qualities had to be attributed to an anti-god. It was the Christians who created the devil.'

Abigail went quiet.

'Does that offend you Miss Abigail?' asked Hester. 'I know what a good church woman you are.'

'No,' Abigail said after a few moments, 'it does not offend me. I am a rational woman and intelligent people value debate and argument. I am not one to discard any opinion out of hand.' She smiled to let the child know her words were genuine, but Hester could tell she was still turning the words over in her mind, checking them out, trying to make sense of them.

'Is that all?' Hester asked.

'Sorry?'

'Nothing more about Isis?'

Abigail focused once more on the child and checked the pages again before shutting the book. 'No. I'm sorry.'

'And that was my only clue. The only name I had. And we've been through most every book in the library,' exclaimed Hester.

Abigail opened her mouth twice but each time she closed it again without speaking. She was looking past Hester's shoulder, staring clear through the shelf of books, when she spoke finally.

'I believe I can get you to any book you choose,' said Abigail carefully, 'but it won't be easy.'

'It wasn't easy getting this far,' said Hester, her words too grown up for the skinny scruff of a child that she looked.

Abigail seemed worried. 'And that is the only reason I contemplate it,' she said. 'I don't know how much the good Lord will thank me for helping you to find out more,' she said slowly, 'because this old religion has fallen from grace itself.'

Hester sensed something and, whatever it was, it pricked the strange memories in her head again.

'Yes?' she asked, tentatively.

'We are talking witchcraft, Hester,' said Abigail.

What Abigail suggested was a trip to the upstairs library. It was, after all, 1958 and the Supreme Court had declared several years before that segregation was unconstitutional in the United States of America. Much of the American Deep South had chosen to ignore this with the sheriffs and county judges the first to defend what they considered to be the superior rights of white Americans. What Abigail had in mind was a deliberate flaunting of local authority by claiming the right to borrow books from the main town library.

'You mean it?' said Hester when she had heard what Abigail had to say, her eyes so big they were set to pop out her head.

'The right is yours by law ... but that may not mean a thing around here,' said Abigail.

'Why didn't you tell me before,' Hester wanted to know.

'Because I don't know yet why I'm telling you even now.'

It was the honest truth. A voice inside Abigail's head was yelling at her to stop. Yet another was pushing her forward. She couldn't for the life of her tell which was the voice of her Lord, a voice she had listened to unfalteringly for thirty-seven years. It was a puzzle all right.

'Listen to me Hester,' she said, taking the other chair from behind her official library desk and placing it next to Hester at the table in the center of the room. Then she took the child's hands in her own.

'There are things I've wanted to tell people in this town since the day I arrived,' Abigail said. 'Have you ever heard of the Supreme Court?'

'Is that the sheriff?'

'In a manner of speaking,' she said, 'but it's higher than the sheriff. It's the law. The highest law in this entire country. And that law has taken a good long look at the Declaration of Independence. You know what that is?'

'Yes ma'am,' said Hester enthusiastically.

Abigail walked over to her desk and came back with a large box file. She took out a newspaper cutting and placed it on the table in front of Hester. The headline read 'Black Monday'.

Hester leaned over the clipping and studied the story. 'May 17 1954. The US Supreme Court ruled the philosophy that all men are created equal is the American way. Henceforth it will be unlawful to maintain schools segregated by race'. Hester looked up.

'Is this true Miss Abigail?'

'It's more than true my dear, it's history,' said Abigail. 'And a fat bit of good it's done you so far,' she said under her breath.

Abigail pulled more newspaper cuttings from her box file and placed them for the child to read.

'At Little Rock, Arkansas, President Eisenhower has dispatched 500 of the 101st Airborne Division, 500 miscellaneous paratroopers and federalized 10,000 men in the Arkansas National Guard as trouble is expected following the abolition of segregation in schools. Warnings have been given by the pro-segregation lobby for the Southern States that blacks are a breeding ground for syphilis and little white girls will be highly susceptible to contracting it if integrated drinking fountains are allowed. The same goes for books, towels and gym clothes if segregation is allowed to be abandoned.' Hester's forehead creased again.

'Does that mean I can go to school here,' she asked.

'It means you can go to the black school as you always could but you live too far out of town. I wouldn't suggest you take on the entire State legislature just yet by trying to get enrolled in the white school, for all the President says you are entitled,' recommended Abigail.

'The drinking fountain?' Hester had admired the town's water fountain since her first trip to the library. Its elaborate wrought iron figure of a cherub gurgled up a spout of crystal water for the white children to gorge on hot dusty days while the black youngsters made do with a rusty standpipe. The iron cherub stood on three circles of white marble, each circle smaller than the one below so even the smallest child could climb up and get within reach of the water. The park keeper, the only colored person allowed in the park, washed and polished up the marble every morning to keep the water and summer dust from mixing to a mud and spoiling the monument; a gift presented some fifty years earlier by a town dignitary most people had forgotten. The standpipe, outside the park gates, rose straight out the ground and was always a quagmire in summer, the sun never managing to dry out the puddled mud from the constant scrabble of children's splashed feet.

'You cannot afford to waste your moment of glory on some drinking fountain,' answered Abigail. 'If we do this, we do it for real. If you are willing Hester, I suggest we try to get you in the upstairs library.'

Hester's stomach went cold as she felt again the disgrace of being marched out the library on her first trip to town. The woman's scream rang in her ears and she burned with shame at the memory she tried to forget.

'They won't let me in,' said Hester after a few moments.

'Maybe they won't,' said Abigail honestly, 'and I can't lie to you that we can truly get you in there, but you have a right by law and it could be time to remind folks round here of that right.'

'If they pick me up and throw me out how will that help to remind them? They'll just laugh.'

'That's exactly what they may do Hester, but I'll be with you and I'll make sure I'm not the only one. If we invite the newspaper men to take photographs of you being carried out then the story may just embarrass them instead, and that could be a victory also.'

The woman and the child looked down at the newspaper cuttings in and around the box. Pictures and stories marking history.

'The newspaper men in these parts are all white,' Hester said simply.

'Then we will invite newspaper men from New York and Chicago if we have to,' decided Abigail.

The idea seemed almost possible when she talked with Abigail in the magic of what she now called 'her library', the dingy basement room in the town that was a lifetime away from her home and three women at the spigot. When she tried to explain it later, to Sissie Jane, it became a stupid and reckless venture even to her own ears.

'Suicide,' I recalls muttering, chipping in my own two cents worth and chewing at the insides of my gums with the few teeth I had left.

Rounded Libby pushed a stick round in the dirt, keeping her eyes fixed on it as she told us she was all for making a stand. That was when Sissie Jane reminded us of Joe, though she never mentioned him roasting in the tree. She just said his name, simply, and let it echo between us. There was a long pause after that.

Chapter 8

RECALLING AN IMPORTANT DAY - JUNE 11th 1958
THE LIBRARY

It was the following morning and Old Loula met the man once more at the same place. He had spent the evening staring at the screen of his laptop, unable still to find a way of starting what he needed to write. The empty beer cans had piled up on the small table until he finally gave up and closed the machine down. Only when he pulled out his small notebook did the words start to flow, creeping out from behind the rocks in his mind. At the moment, his and Old Loula's stories were wildly different but he thought they would converge soon. He had long been haunted by things he didn't understand. Now was his chance to work it out.

* * *

Old Loula had promised the young man she would tell Hester's story but there were some parts she found difficult. After she was settled she continued where she had left off the day before.

Now I'd like this to be known from the start, she told him, I never did think that library idea was a good one. I won't lay claim to no psychic powers or nothing, that was Hester's department not mine, but I did have a bad feeling about that day, June 11th 1958, and I was proved right.

Abigail, true to her word, had found us a sea of newspaper photographers from the State and beyond. As soon as the folks from out of town got interested, the local press had to cover it too, to put their side of the story. They would rather have ignored us altogether and let the sheriff take over the affair in peace and quiet because if a story like this got in the papers then every Tom, Dick and Harry would be out challenging the way of it. But if the big boys was going to make the kid into a hero it was up to decent reporting Southern press to put the record straight. It was Lee Grant ran the Evening Standard, covering the three towns in the area, and he checked with the sheriff exactly the best course of action the paper might take. The sheriff reckoned if Lee had his photographer look out for just the right shot, some black raising a hand at a white woman or some such, then they could work on the story between them to get the angle right. Lee assured the sheriff he would get the shot, knowing he had just the collection to fall back on if need be because he kept a file of such photographs ready to be used. There was a great one of Jed, the blacksmith's boy, looking for all the world like he was spitting on the pretty red shoes of a blond cherub of a little girl about three years old. He wasn't, of course. Old Jed was just bending to pick up the hind leg of a workhorse and he was whistling, as always. The little girl was stood behind and something must of frightened her, most likely the horse, because the look on her sweet face was pure panic. I know on account of Lee used that photo some time later. The horse might have been in the photograph to start with but it had been cut out. Lee Grant had a whole file load of library shots just waiting for a good story to snap them up.

The day was well publicized and Hester was ready in the town more than an hour early. Our Libby was with her, shuffling on her bunions and the heat dripping off her great fat arms, and Libby's daughter and grandchildren. Even Jesse, the boy on the bicycle, who swore not to tease Hester the whole day if she would let him come along and maybe get in the papers also.

Mr Big from the mezzanine floor was there too.

It was planned that Abigail, as the librarian, would go in first but as it turned out the crowd of objectors was so strong none of them could make it up the steps. Abigail started the speech she had prepared while she, Hester and Libby held hands and tried to press forward. Libby is the size of at least two women even though she is quite short so you would think her weight would gain them some advantage but it was not so easy. Sissie Jane was just behind them, towering over the sheriff's men that stood between them and the crowd. Cameras was going off all around and the photographers pushed in from all sides, ready to get the best shot. That was when the first rock was thrown. Hester tried hard to keep a hold of Abigail's hand but the librarian was being stretched in two as the crowd pushed Libby and Hester aside. The steps above them throbbed with town folk determined to preserve their library and their entire way of life and it seemed to Hester they was being pushed back faster than they could press forward. Hester was the only one small enough to duck under the legs and once she lost hold of Abigail's hand she weaved her way through the chaos to those large carved doors. She hesitated only a moment before slipping inside.

It was oddly quiet inside the library because everyone else was on the steps. The silent books all around held her history and she wanted to stay in the cool room until she had read them all. She had done what she set out to do and made it inside the library, but no one was there to witness it. Outside, several people was kicked to the ground and most of the onlookers then pulled back out of fright. The photographers was the only ones jostling for position then, waiting for the picture that would please their editors and make them famous on the front page of their papers. They would not be disappointed.

After just a few minutes Hester went back through the library doors to the heat outside and squirmed down to where Libby was helping Abigail who had a cut knee from falling on the stone steps. She was just in time to see one of the sheriff's men stand over the two women and lift his baton high above his head. It all slowed down, so the scene in front of Hester's eyes played in unreal time and the man's lips moved long before the sound came out. He swung that stick up and round and down on Abigail's head before the words caught up and Hester heard the shriek:

'Bitch!' he cried.

It wasn't until later again that the crack of hard wood finally rang out from the librarian's skull. It was all so disjointed. Heater's own words had left her lips as she was scampering down the steps, trying to tell Libby and Abigail she had been inside the library doors, but the sound never reached her own ears until Abigail was crumpled slowly down to the ground.

'I did it,' Hester heard herself say.

'Quiet girl,' said Libby.

They both looked down at the blood pooling into Libby's ample lap from Abigail's split skull.

*   *   *

Hester got no books that day Abigail died, said Old Loula. What she did get when the stories in the newspapers finally settled down was a compromise. The main library arranged for the catalogues to be borrowed by downstairs. She could have her choice of two books each time and they would be waiting for her the next visit. It gave Hester a way to find the information she wanted but that was no kind of triumph when it would always be tainted with Abigail's death. But maybe she owed it to the librarian to keep right on looking and that is what she did.

We are talking witchcraft, Abigail had said, so that is what Hester read. Methodically, she ate up every scrap of writing the library could find her.

'Did you know,' Hester says to me one day, 'nine million people in Europe was accused of witchcraft and died?' Hester had been reading them books you see. 'And the Americans killed some too. See here,' she said, and pointed to some words from a book she had brung out to the spigot. 'They was burned, hanged or tortured to death. The English and Americans preferred hanging but the Scots and Europeans took to burning folk at the stake. The old religion,' that was how Hester spoke of it now, 'the old religion went back through 25,000 years of worship. To Paleolithic times.'

Paleolithic was a word that took her a time to get her mind and tongue round. Me too, but I still recall it. There was many long and important sounding words she found in them books. She told me she felt her soul tracing itself back over the dust of 25,000 years. For a child of 11 years, that was a lot of dust, I said to her. And most of them books told only the story of how that religion died and gave no clue to its life, which was what she was after.

Hester kept up her reading, even when the words made no sense to her. In fourteen hundred and somesuch Pope Innocent VIII produced a Bull against witches, it said. I remember, you see? Hester was curious about the bull. Was it like the lions' den and the Christians, she wanted to know? She had imagined a cross between that and a Spanish bullfight, Rome and Spain seeming so alike to a young girl in America. She hoped it wasn't too awful for the witch women. Better than burning, she told me.

Fourteen hundred and something, said another book, and two German monks wrote this famous anti-witchery book 'Malleus Maleficarum'. Translated it meant Hammer of the Witches. Hester imagined a giant hammer, something with pistons and machinery, steam-driven and mechanical, that smelt of factories and trains as it smashed down on the heads of innocent women who all had the faces of Sissie Jane, Libby and me probably. She read on. The mass hysteria that followed after the book was published – she knew what hysteria was because she saw the screaming of a poor woman when her child was killed by a horse kick right in the center of town and Hester and the other children was told not to look because it was just a woman with hysteria, but they all saw the blood and knew – the mass hysteria meant everyone wanted rid of the witches. They hunted out them witches for nearly 300 years, with whole villages destroyed just to get at one or two blamed for witchcraft. The book said folk was crying 'destroy them all...the Lord will know his own' and all them innocent people was killed.

Hester asked me about Sissie Jane, a woman who always claimed to be on first name terms with God, and we wondered how Sissie might have kept her faith under a witches hammer. Hester pondered it for a while, twisting her small spike braids between her fingers while she tried to work it out, but finally deciding it was all beyond her comprehension. She went back to puzzling the heavy book in front of her.

Then the book talked about what happened after the Reformation, and Hester could not find out what that word meant either, but it told her that after this Reformation many who had been working in the monasteries because they was poor, old or deformed, became outcasts and had no place to go. It seems like they just took themselves off to places where no other folk lived and set to living in forests and swamps where nobody else cared to go. Hester said could I imagine it but it seems I did not have the pictures in my head that she kept.

She read to me about some Witchunter General as earned twenty dollars or twenty shillings each time he found hisself a witch. It seems to me he would be finding plenty of witches if that was the rate of pay. I can see the temptation. Matthew Hopkins his name was and it seems he was a mean piece of work.

I recall she read to me about some Archbishop, in 1586 it was and I know that date for a fact for it is the very reverse of the year my grandmother was so proud of telling me she was born. I was born in 1856 Little Loula, she always said, and a free woman fore I was knee high, though whether that is a fact or not I could not tell you. She was not good with numbers, my grandmother. Anyhow, this Archbishop decided some witches had caused the winter to be bad and he got people to confess. They didn't just say it was them as done it, he had to torture them first until they agreed it must of been their fault. One hundred and twenty-seven men and women was burned to death for that cold winter. And they wasn't even black.

Hester told me all this for most other folks was too busy to listen. She brought some of them books home, though it seemed a sacrilege to read them old great words in the dust at the spigot and so much more reverent in the cool of the library room under the bare bulb at her table in the center of the room. When Libby looked over her shoulder one morning at the spigot and saw about the Malleus Maleficarum, she asked for the book to read. It wasn't until the next day Hester got it back. I watched as Hester heard Libby telling Sissie Jane about it.

'Obsessed they were,' she hissed, 'obsessed with ... you know'. There was a hushed pause and a raising of eyebrows between the two of them as Sissie stooped down to get nearer to Libby for a good whisper.

'Sex?' asks Sissie Jane.

'And them both monks,' finished Libby.

'Dominican monks,' chipped in Hester, though she had no idea what that might be.

I stayed a ways back as most times, preferring to keep my nose out of it for fear of being called a gossip. Those times Hester and I had together was private. I would not let on to the others that I had a interest in the child. I could see Hester was waiting for more scandal but none was coming. Libby went back to the main task of drawing water, the faded cotton of her dress stretched tight over her great back and wet with the sweat of the day. Sissie Jane walked away without another word, her dress hanging gaunt and shapeless as the body beneath it.

Hester decided to take the book under the shade of a tree and decipher it some more. The words were that long and her grasp of reading still so fragile it took a whole lot of effort. She was fascinated mostly by the words of the old religion, her old religion she called it. 'An it harm none, do what thou wilt'. Hester said it was a very Christian creed to live by; do what you want, believe what you want, as long as it don't harm nobody else. She decided this must be the meaning of the words but it still seemed all wrong to me. Surely it was the Christians would say something like that, not the witch women.

What puzzled Hester most was the hangings. Several books told her witches was hanged in England, not burned, and she was sure her past lay in the pink part, those English pages of the atlas. It was only in Europe and Scotland they burned her people, several books agreed on that point, so it was a puzzle all right. I said as I couldn't shed no more light on it myself so Hester waited to see would Sissie Jane come back to the spigot.

But it seems Sissie had her fill of water for one day. At last she asked Libby for her opinion. As always I just kept my head down and made like I wasn't paying no mind.

'If that was in the books, in the libary,' said Libby, 'then it must be true, I reckon. If hanging it says then hanging it was, and not burning.'

'It said they never burned witches in England, that it was the custom to hang them,' said Hester, 'but I am certain I was never hanged. It's fire that frightens me.'

'Well you never drowned, that's for sure,' said Libby. 'I never did see a child so taken with the water as you Hester. You been swimming in that crick since you could walk, for all we told you to keep away.'

'All the friends that ever I had are round me when I'm in water. She told me never to fear it,' said Hester.

'What?' Libby was getting deaf even back then.

'Water,' repeated Hester.

'Who told you that?'

'I don't recall,' said Hester.

'No folk would tell a water baby like you not to be afraid of water,' said Libby.

'That's strange,' said Hester.

'Sure is.'

'No, I meant ... well ... what I said just then,' Hester looked at Libby, as if she might understand. 'I know who told me not to be afraid.'

Libby saw the importance. 'Yes?' she asked kindly.

'I know her name somewhere. It won't come out but it's there. Beginning with H, like mine,' said Hester. 'And she takes my hand as she says it, my bad hand, the small one, the white one, and I am never afraid after that.'

'White hand?' asked Libby, surprised.

'Yes,' said Hester.

'Not even brown?'

'No. So very pale. As if no sun shines on it even. I feel sorry for the hand. Not just because it is small, but because it is so pale,' said Hester.

'You been at your pappy's gin still young Hester?' asked Libby.

Chapter 9

Hester knew when to expect trouble from Solomon, maybe before he knew it himself. It was when he told her how she looked so like her mother that the fear started to grow. It gripped her insides, turning her cold. Already Solomon touched her but there would be more, she felt sure, and she waited for it to happen.

One morning her eyes blinked open, her thoughts already awake in her head. She saw him looking over at her, the power of his stare crossing the distance between his big marriage bed under the window and her small trundle cot against the wall. He said nothing for a long time but she saw his hand moving under the thin, worn blanket. She thought to turn her back against him but didn't know if it would help. There didn't seem any way she could leave the room without slipping out from under her own quilt and she had been careful these last months to rise before he woke. Today she was too late.

Her breasts had started to grow in that childish way, with the brown disc round her nipples swelling soft and hot, sticking out under her cotton dress and aching with the growing. What with that and her legs rising like stilts, pushing her further from the ground and nearer the faces of the adults she had looked up to for so long, Hester knew her body was dangerous now.

'What you staring at girl?' Solomon asked.

She wouldn't answer him.

'Come over here,' he told her.

She tried to keep every muscle in her body still.

'You do as you bin told,' he repeated, 'as a good child should.'

She blinked.

'You come right now and you bring the strap with you and take your punishment for disobeying your elders and betters,' Solomon said slowly.

She slid off the trundle sideways, keeping her drawers and bare chest covered by the quilt, standing stock still, waiting for the order to come again.

He beckoned her with a slight tilt of his head and she stooped and took the belt from his pants before inching towards the big bed. She held it up to him, keeping the quilt around her with the other hand.

He took the belt and laid it on the pallet. He would use it later to tie her hands because she struggled too much. For now he just pulled her onto the bed and placed her right hand over himself. He thought a hand would be enough for him but this time it wouldn't be. He wanted to push her head under the blanket but the thought only made him want her more. He untied her from the knot of quilt she had wrapped herself in and pulled her drawers down past her knees before he explored slowly between her legs. No hair grew there yet. Nature had given her no defense.

When he tied her hands he was quite gentle, pulling the strap through the metal buckle and finding a hole already punched which would keep her thin arms tight and out the way behind her back. She turned her head in shame as he checked the small growth where her breasts would be. Then he ran his hand down her and spread her legs, locking them open with his knees. Her drawers got in the way and he bent over her to pull them free and throw them to the floor.

It was the first time he had entered her and the surprise was almost worse than the pain. Hester had never understood before the connection between his hardness and her own body although she had long understood that his power had something to do with her own thighs and the place between her legs. In the past he had been content with touching her and touching himself. This was the first time the idea of their two bodies tried to make some sense in her mind, but all she could feel was the horror of it and the blood oozing down between her legs.

It didn't take more than a few minutes because he had waited a long time.

Hester could not believe that anyone else had ever done this before.

Chapter 10

Hester was surprised nobody saw the difference in her next day, said Old Loula. I know this for she has since told me the most part of it, and I can figure the rest even if you think I look like a stupid old woman. Anyroad, Hester come to the spigot as before but it seems we carried on as normal. She sat with us three old women and imagined us all in bed with men, being pierced at that most private part, and wondered if we too felt tainted like she did. Try as she might she just could not wash away the smell or stop the wetness from drenching her drawers. She looked at the faces in turn and wondered if it was this had turned us old. Suddenly she wanted to check her own face for change but first she forced herself to sit quiet at the spigot, imagining her life here among the women, not as before in the body of a child but as a part of womanhood. Was this why the men in history had killed their women as witches, after they had spoiled them?

Libby had a mirror in her cabin but Hester waited until she could get to the crick to see Sally. There she inspected her face from every angle but the difference in her seemed not to show on the outside. Solomon's guilty secret was tucked safe between her legs, she found. Perhaps Sally saw something had changed and maybe she didn't mention it because it would not have helped. As Hester sat at Sally's kitchen table, the mirror in front of her, Sally walked behind and squeezed her shoulders, nestling her own chin into Hester's neck.

'Keep smiling girl. I don't know what other advice to give you,' she said and then walked away to put on fresh coffee.

That was as near as they came to discussing Solomon.

Hester returned to her books once more, searching for a better life in her head than the one she found round her. History filled as many of her waking moments as her chores would allow but many of the facts seemed distant and unhelpful. She knew she was getting nearer and nearer to the pink place on the map but at the same time she needed a key to let her into the world of the pale girl with a shriveled hand and leg. She tried to make sense of the words she was reading, though it was all wars and taxes, nothing at all about real people and their lives.

Hester read while the supper boiled over and ran dry. At night she accepted the beatings or caresses that came her way and waited for Solomon to fall asleep so she could creep out the room and read again in the light of a candle.

The words buzzed around Hester's head as she tried to make sense of it all. The Catholics and the Pope were on the same side, that bit was easy, and the English Queen Elizabeth left the Catholics and said she was in charge of her own church, Church of England. It was getting more difficult after that because the Protestants didn't like the Catholics but they weren't too fond of the Church of England either, and sometimes they was called Puritans. She still didn't understand why they were all dead against the old religion, the worship of love and the earth, the religion she felt closest to. There were more words too; the Huguenots were foreigners, and papists was another word for Catholics. Church of England and Anglican seemed to be the same thing but still no one seemed to like the Protestants.

Not much of it was relevant to Hester until one evening she found a passage which gave her a glimpse of the real people of the time. She had been up for hours and was fighting to keep her eyes from shutting. She wanted to finish the book before it was due back in the library next day.

She read of the civil war, 1642. This book said the people were angry with having a war. It meant they couldn't trade. Soldiers from both sides were fighting in the fields, destroying crops, taking the farm animals without paying. And if that wasn't bad enough they burned the houses after they stole all they wanted and made the men join up as soldiers. Some men, the ones with brains, got together with clubs and fought to keep the war out of their towns and villages. To pay for the war the taxes went up and then nobody was happy.

Suddenly Hester could feel these people round her. This part of the book was right; the people themselves were angry with the war. They knew that fighting and even the winning would not benefit them, they were only the ones getting wounded and killed. Whoever won or lost, nothing would improve their own lives. It was like listening to the talking of folk that lived in cabins around her. These people in the war were suddenly very close to Hester, their voices half heard, just like as a child drifts off to sleep while adults talk on. Hester felt at home. Heliotrope, her herb mother, told her not to fear because the water would keep them safe.

She decided not to worry about the war or the witch hunter. Heliotrope was always right. Maybe she was right about the water too, although Poppy had always been afraid of water. As Hester's eyelids finally closed and her head came to rest on the table her hair lay just inches away from the small stub of candle.

Chapter 11

O ld Loula listened to some young children playing nearby and tried to recall the days when Hester was young in body and soul.

I may not be in a position to relay Hester's thoughts exactly, she told him, but I certainly know she near set light to her own hair that night. It was the awful smell of singeing hair as woke her up and if ever you have had the misfortune to smell human hair burning then you will understand the panic it put her into. It don't need saying that it reminded her of the day they cut her brother Joe from out that tree.

Hester's hair had caught from the candle she was reading by, and it woke her up real quick and as she beat at the brittle ends of her hair it sent sparks showering round her in the near dark and frightened her again. She ran to the pail of water that stood on the floor by the washbowl and flopped onto the ground to dunk her head in. Most likely the burnt bits were out by now but she had took a fright and wanted to be sure.

Her head dripping, she went back to the table and tried to get her heart to stop thumping like that.

'That you Hester?' said Solomon, standing in the doorway to the bedroom. 'Whatever time you call this?' he asked her. 'If it's them damn books again I swear I'll burn 'em,' he said.

You see, the library book Hester was reading had a song in it that told the women's story, or so she said. As soon as it was daylight she ran to the spigot and she couldn't believe no one was there. I was always at the spigot, not having much else to occupy my time. Some called it idleness, I know that, but I did as many chores as needed to be done and that was enough to my way of thinking. You can only get a cabin to a certain state of cleanness and the remainder of the effort is pretty near wasted as far as I can see, but there you have it. Sissie Jane was one of them 'cleanliness is next to Godliness' freaks and she passed most of her time on her knees with a scrubbing brush in her hands for her efforts. Maybe I had more respect for my enamel pail than to have it full of dirty water at all hours of the day, that's all I'm saying. Still, on that morning Hester was way early and found no one at the spigot so she ran all the way to Sissie Jane's, breathless with the power of the song. It needed singing, she explained.

Could Sissie Jane do a tune? It was asking a lot, the melting of English folklore into the field holler blues that was all Sissie Jane knew of, but it worked. Better than you would think.

Sissie Jane hummed and crooned her way through the song, egged on as Hester prompted the words that Sissie could not read. Those who have no call to rely on books always have good memories and Sissie had the words in her head in no time.

'... In a war against the women
Who's power they feared,
Nine million European women died ...
A holocaust of tears ...'

'Nine million,' breathed Hester. 'Can it really have been nine million?'

'Most like they made it up to fit the song,' grumbled Sissie Jane, annoyed that her singing was interrupted yet again and her just getting the hang of it too.

'No,' said Hester. 'There was many that died; I know it was a powerful lot of people. But get to the next part,' she said, chivvying Sissie along. 'You must sing the next part.'

Hester helped Sissie with the words, picking up the rhythm herself, living the words as she had for so long already. Knowing them for a truth she felt inside her. Hester was now very close to the girl in her head, so close she felt she knew her.

'...The tale is told of women
Who were dying to be free,
Who by the hundreds held together
Choosing death from the sea ...'

* * *

That was the start to tell the truth, the beginning of a time when little Hester come to life and started to understand the other girl in her head, Poppy. Suddenly little Hester become so animated it was hard keeping her quiet for she would come rushing out to the spigot most any time of day or evening and tell some new part of the story that was unfolding in front of her. 'Loula,' she would say to me, 'you won't hardly believe what happen now,' then she would sit up on the seat beside me and if I was alone, because I never will look too encouraging if Sissie or Libby is about on account of them sniping at me which they tend to do saying as how I is a old grump, them times when we was alone I would let little Hester sit right up close and she would let me in on a history from her head. She called it that sometimes, a history.

Of course she told parts of the tale to others as well and I'm not saying as how I was the only one as was privy to the story but sometimes I feel I was the only person apart from Hester who pieced together the fragments of recollection and found a story in them. And for all that Sissie Jane was more like a mother to the child and Libby the one fussing over her, in my own quiet way maybe I played my part in living that life with her and none of the others any the wiser as it became our small secret, Hester and me. Our two souls are not as different as it might appear but I would not let on to the others. If the girl chose to live in her head rather than outside of it then that was fine by me and a thing I could understand. She lives there most of the time these days and that is the trouble with it from most folk's point of view for she seldom goes out now but chooses to sit at the spigot, vacant and staring and mostly deaf to what people say to her. Course, she is a grown woman herself now and her hair gone gray too. But I consider it a privilege to say as I understand her and why she chooses to keep her thoughts elsewhere.

Like I said, there was times, secret times between her and me, when we would gather together the fragments of Poppy's life and make some sense of it. To my mind they was the best times for Hester and they wasn't to last long, poor child.

I would like to tell all I know, which maybe is not too much but it is all I could learn of Hester before that terrible thing happen to her and set her mind to staying elsewhere. If only I could figure a way to tell Poppy's story, for I am not a storyteller mind and I could not tell it as well as Hester told me, then I would certainly do so. But I do not rightly know how to do it for when she spoke of Poppy, Hester would get sucked right into the story and suddenly she wasn't saying 'Poppy said' or 'Poppy saw', but 'I say' and 'I see' like she had truly become the other girl in her

96

head and it was happening to her right there and then with some of the words old fashion and not like we use at all. And her voice would change too, like when she spoke of Poppy as a young girl then her voice would be childlike and the words primitive and hesitant. Yet the times she told of Poppy grown up to a young woman, well then Hester's voice would sound more grown up than you could imagine coming from that scrap of a girl as sat on that seat next to me at the spigot.

What did you say your name was? Old Loula asked the man. Joseph, he told her. Now that is a coincidence, she said.

That's about it really, said Old Loula, picking up her pail and heading back to her cabin for the evening. Except that wasn't it at all. Joseph had voices too, crystal clear stories put into his head when he was so small he never noticed them slipping in. They formed a part of him like finding out how to walk and talk. Now he was finally beginning to understand where his nightmares came from.

Chapter 12

Joseph, the listener, went back to his hotel room and placed the small leather case carefully on the bed and opened it, pulling out a half written manuscript. Then he checked his notebook, looking for an answer in the words he had scribbled as Old Loula spoke.

He had waited a long time to see how Hester's story wrapped around the other one, the one he knew very well. The two things seemed so hard to weld together, the life of Hester herself and that of Poppy. He didn't remember much of Hester as a child, just the presence of her sitting with him on the green rug in his mother's cabin confiding her stories to him. What he knew more was the life of Poppy, which he grasped as fully as any child brings to life the words of a fairy story.

Joseph poured himself a drink from the mini-bar in his room, cleared the case onto the floor and stretched out on the bed. It now seemed an impossible task to do what he intended, to come back South and build the real Hester into his book. And to find out about the eyes. He picked up the manuscript and looked at what he had written so long ago, the part he knew, the life of Poppy. Did he really recall the rest, or had he embellished it? Perhaps he didn't know any more. But the more he looked at the words the less they seemed to mean.

* * *

POPPY'S STORY BY JOSEPH G JEFFERSON.

CHAPTER 1

Page 1.
That morning in 1628, the day of the child's birth, the child they would later call Poppy because of a poppy-red birthmark on her thigh, Heliotrope the witch woman took a handful of ferns and covered the serving girl's face, noticing the cold blue-white of the young skin against her own chapped hands and knowing what a feeble gesture it was anyway when the poor girl was dead now and beyond her care. Yet she deserved to be in a bed with a blanket

pulled up to hide out the world from her spiritless eyes, thought Heliotrope. Well, she'd done her best by her at the last, although the thought nagged that she should have known more, known the girl Rose would run off away from the women's huts in the clearing just as the baby was ready to come.

And she was still puzzled to find Rose had died when she least expected it. There seemed no reason, she was young and strong, she never bled the way some women did, but it seemed she gave up. A little early, thought Heliotrope sternly as she moved away from the mother and put her attentions to the baby. She gave up a little early, she thought. Before the child was quite born. She was worried now, for the child. It looked up at her, quiet and waiting, as pale and cold as its mother and she wasn't sure how to warm it. March was a damp month, and not a good time to be one hour old in the marshes, wrapped only in a shawl.

A seagull squawked at them from the mud flats and Heliotrope cuddled the baby girl into the great folds of her chest to crawl as best she could into the small shelter where the girl Rose had been living this past week. The shelter she'd dug into the mud bank to protect her from the prying eyes and cruel tongues of hypocrites. It would have served him right, thought Heliotrope, the master at his grand manor house, if Rose had stayed at her serving work and let them all see her rising apron. Still, it would have remained her own shame and not his, a funny thing that had never been properly explained as far as Heliotrope was concerned. It was him that should have known better, master of Manningtree Manor, for Rose was only a babe herself, not sixteen or so she doubted. She looked down at the body of the dead serving girl, twisted a little unnaturally, her head half obscured with leaves and her damp yellow hair matted into the mud. A small pool of blood seeped out from between her legs and was soaking away with the rain. There was barely room for the two of them in here ... three of them, corrected Heliotrope.

'Not that you're big enough to warrant your own space,' she said aloud. Funny how you carry on talking to small babes and dumb animals even when it can do no good, she thought.

But he had a grand house, the master of Manningtree Manor,

and money, and it was only the girl's task to serve him, as well she did it seemed, her being his servant. And these last months she had been in hiding with Heliotrope and the others who valued life for its own sake, never caring where it came from, knowing the soul was a different matter altogether. They were happy with her there, in their huts on the outskirts of the town, expecting her to stay while she waited for the child to come. Why did she run off like that? It had taken days to find her. And not easy days, with Huguenots being hounded through the mud flats and anyone about their business likely to be rounded up and claimed an enemy. These were certainly strange times.

Heliotrope pulled her own clothes closer round the baby for warmth and crouched even further back into the shelter out of the biting wind. She took one of the small hands in her own and squeezed it for a response, waiting for its fist to grasp one of her fingers as newborn babies always did. She half expected it wouldn't. No. Nothing. So why was she so disappointed? The hand fell away limp. She was worried now that the labor had lasted all those days since Rose had disappeared, that the girl had stayed alone in this shelter, trying to get her baby born.

Not that it was a shelter even, these ferns and rushes lapping over the ledge formed by the roots above, this being a dip in the bank that the girl had clawed out a little more. Just enough room to sit huddled against the wet mud wall that still supported the ledge above it. The child's hand was icy now. There wasn't time to bury the girl yet, or she'd be burying them both together, mother and child. Heliotrope settled for pulling the girl's apron up to cover her face better, then she got up and sprinkled over some brown stalks from the year before and whispered a few words to the wind. That would have to suffice for now, she told herself, until she could be back.

She stepped out of her petticoats and lifted the child again, wrapping it as best she could in the flannel, over and over, binding it, then blowing warm on its face from her own breath, watching the eyes open again and stare at her. She held it close to her for warmth, tucking it under her deep breasts and knowing she would have no milk to give it, that it would be a wonder if it lived long enough for her to find any. As she bent to cover the face with her own, to nuzzle some warmth back into it and make a windbreak of herself, she hoped she might be wrong. There could be life there.

She stepped out from the bank and the wind lashed salt in her face as she made for the path back to Mistley Thorn. It would be a long walk with the sea spraying at her and no shawl to wear, the wind whipping her skirt against her stout bare legs.

❊ ❊ ❊

Poppy remembered the day of her birth. The sea never came tossing in with waves but crept in like a thief over the shallow mud flats.

She could see it now, the day of her birth, the day her Yarb Mother Heliotrope refused to send her back to wait for another life. She pulled her from her mother's dead body, away from the bright light where she had waited for so long, to the chill of the gray Essex coast. Poppy wondered how many times she had felt this. The sea here had been gray forever.

The salt marshes and creeks round Foulness saw things to make the toes curl on a corpse. But not her mother's corpse. Poppy was aware of her, Rose, who had left life just as she was entering it. Her toes were not curled and there would be little now to surprise her, neither the Essex marsh gray water nor the smugglers it watched, hearing the tales of ghouls and wicces to keep the folk in their beds of a foggy night and as far away as possible from the four and twenty ponies trotting through the dark, laces for a lady, letters for a clerk, not to mention the parson's brandy. The salt marsh mist saw as far as Manningtree and Mistley Thorn too, where religions of peace must kill one another to prove which is right, or stronger, or both, that is what Poppy's Yarb Mother would tell her as she grew. The Blackwater River knew, as it crept its black watery way down to the Island and the sea. It knew the Wiccan Crede, the oldest religion of them all ... an it harm none, do what you will ... do what you will as long as it doesn't harm anyone else. Not that the Huguenots or the gypsies were ready to listen to wicces' telling of old ways. Few lived in the marshlands, and those that did had need to. The law was invisible there. Old Johnny, the ague, was the only thing to thrive. And Poppy, of course, if you could call it thriving, with one hand born withered and one leg that would never keep pace with the other. It would not be her Yarb Mother's fault, for all her yarbs or herbs that would be called forth to cure the affliction and would always fail, it could never be her fault that Poppy stayed too long in her dead mother's body and came out, when eventually she did, a little damaged. Poppy could feel it, you see. Before the damp chill of Essex finally clothed her and made her small lungs want to cry out, she could feel the white light engulfing her again and believed she could withdraw once more and wait her turn to be born in a different time.

It was lucky for Poppy that the wicces would accept her when her true family would not. Wicce was the female name and wicca the male, but those who were afraid called them witches. Witan was the council of the wise ones. Her Yarb Mother Heliotrope was a wise one, an awesome woman, as any would tell you. There would be plenty of time for Poppy to gain knowledge in this later. To start she would have to grow, as best she could, and with two limbs dragging their heels as far as growing was concerned. She would live with those they called the wicces because her own mother Rose lay dead in front of her, with no curl to her toes at all because even death had not surprised her, and because Poppy's father had already disowned her. Abandoned her before they could be acquainted. She could not blame her lack of family on her disability then, although she would always wonder if ... if she had been born both whole and male whether her father might have reconsidered. It would be true one day that he would become aware there was no heir to his name and would take his sister's son into his house and consider him as his own. But Poppy would never wish to be a male child although there would be many moments when she may crave the completeness of her left arm and leg. The other reason her mother, her birth mother Rose, not her Yarb Mother, had not been surprised by death, and therefore her toes did not curl, was because she expected nothing better. She was a hard working serving girl, or had been until that day, and she it was who had allowed her employer, Poppy's father, to conceive her. Surely, to conceive was to form an idea of something in one's mind? Obviously Poppy did not live up to the concept he had in mind and was not what he envisaged and, besides, the idea may have been his, and formed in his mind, but that is not where he planted it. He gave it to more fertile grounds. And quickly forgot about it. Funny, then, that conception had more to do with premeditation than the physical transfer of sperm to egg.

She would grow, Poppy decided. It was the only thing she could do now. The white light had receded and left her cold and damp in an Essex marsh. It was her destiny, she decided. To grow. Her right side quicker than her left. At times, her affliction seeming greater than at others. The angle, too, being a factor. Time and space. When she would grow quickly, gangling from toddler to child, from chubby girlhood to willowy adolescence, that was when it would notice most, her growing efforts channeled to the one side only. Eventually the tardy half of her catching up a little and the difference fading. And the way you looked at her, that is, if you cared to, could make a difference. Obviously she would always be best from the right, worst from the left, but almost anything would better than straight on, when you could see both sides and compare. Yes, even the view from the left would beat the one from straight on. Poppy would never like folk to see her like that. It would lead to a strange preoccupation of hers, to keep always on the move. You would rarely find her still. But that is not to say she would move fast at all. The faster she would go, the more the limp, so she must take care at all times with the speed.

You might wonder how she would be able to see herself from the outside, as others would see her, as if she was to spend her life down at the pond, gazing in for her reflection at various angles, to check if this, or that, was more flattering or less harmful. It would be easier than pond gazing. Whenever she was born she found she could leave herself and take a view from the outside, although this always faded with time and she lost control of it, only able to see herself at odd moments rather than at will. It would always amaze her that others were not able to do the same. Had they never been able to, or had they lost the knack as they had grown older? Even her Yarb Mother Heliotrope, who knew everything, could not see herself, although she knew about Poppy. There were a few compensations then for her ugly, crippled body, except that all she could see of herself was an ugly, crippled body. Oh, well.

Taken at the right angle then, not too fast or slow, at the right time in her life, you might not even have noticed her affliction. And the lighting had to be favorable. It would be favorable that fateful night. Light enough for him to see Poppy's face, he would say, yet dark enough to make her beautiful. It was a word Nathaniel would be free with, beautiful, but Poppy knew she would not hear it repeated later, if he took what he wanted. For you see, Nathaniel, her cousin, was not like Tom who loved her. He did not care for others, only for what others could give to him, what he could take from them. Tom was the one that knew the meaning of beautiful. Beauty was something you gave, not something you took. Why, then, would Nathaniel have this hold over Poppy? She could hear the words already, echoing across the sixteen years she had not yet lived. It frightened her to hear it before she started this new life.

She was being born for greater things, she thought. That's what Heliotrope, her Yarb Mother, would say in time. That is what she would mutter, first to herself, when Poppy told her what Nathaniel her cousin wanted of her. What gives him the right, she would demand brandishing the soup ladle, spinning round from the fire so quickly that the broth would spill on Tabby's tail and send her off meowing.

The question would not be asked of anyone in particular, it would not be that kind of question, but Sarah Fletcher, good old Sarah, how Poppy longed to grow so she could meet with her, Sarah would catch it and throw back an answer. She would walk into the clearing, Poppy could see her already, so small when she stood beside Heliotrope, bony and withered, her peaky face sad despite the smile she would always wear, gaunt against Heliotrope's ruddy cheeks. Poppy could see her already, walking into the clearing, following her own voice.

'He be a man,' Sarah would say, wiping her hands on her apron as she had the habit of doing even when they are already dry, 'and besides, he was born in wedlock. He thinks that gives him the right.'

'The right to take a girl of his choosing until he chooses not to?' Heliotrope would ask.

But it was the way things had always worked, and Poppy knew the strength Nathaniel had in the one, being a man, and the weakness she had in the other, her father never marrying her mother, nor intending to. Like Nathaniel, her father had felt he could take what he wanted for free.

But it was not that night yet. It was 1628, the day of Poppy's birth, and she had her growing to do, albeit in stages, the right followed slowly by the left.

Poppy dwelt, instead, on Manningtree and Mistley Thorn, where she would grow. Manningtree was the larger, the grander, where she was conceived and where her mother served, in as grand a house as there was in those miserable parts. The weather was bad and so nothing very grand lived or was built around there, the Essex marshes being almost uninhabited because of the ague which was a marsh fever. The clergy and the gentry knowing better than to get themselves a living there.

Mistley Thorn was the more interesting, one mile further along the River Stour, along the estuary. Towards the south was a maze of marshlands. Tendring Hundred they called it. Poppy would always like the sound of that name.

The ague was called Old Johnny and there was a good cure for it for those who knew these things. You took a spider and rolled it all in cobwebs until it was a round pill for swallowing. That was the best way. Some would not take it though, and kept it on the outside where it could not do so much good. If they would not swallow the spider then they must place it in a nutshell and hang it around their neck in a bag of black silk. That would work too, but it was still best to take it inside. And you really could not taste it if the cobweb wrapping was good and tight. If we are to live in a place seething with ague, then we needs must eat spiders, that is what her Yarb Mother, Heliotrope, would say.

There was an inn at Mistley, facing both the estuary and the round pond. The Thorn Inn it was. And Poppy would become very fond of it during her life in Essex. Mistletoe grew in the tree just to the right of the inn, as it did in the woods behind the town. There. Now it sounded like a cozy village and it wasn't at all, but a noisy busy place with boats at the quay and dirty sailors falling into, out of, and over, at the Thorn Inn. Manningtree rogues and Mistley malcontents. That's what they called them. Shipping wasn't everything. There was smuggling too.

Enough of Mistley Thorn for now. Poppy must grow.

Poppy had yet to grow, and yet already she saw her fate in front of her, waiting for her to live this new life when she knew it must end with a walk into the water. We must hold hands, Heliotrope would tell her, tell them all sixteen years later, hold hands as we walk together into the water. United. No Hopkins to divide us. The water will cool us, she would say. Cool the fire of accusations.

Hopkins, the Witchunter General, would come to find them with his list of names. He would have her name, Poppy knew, after Nathaniel had claimed her for a witch. She would offer to flee from Mistley and Manningtree before he came but Heliotrope and the others would say it was no use, that he had them all marked down for a pricking and a hanging, that he would strip them and paw at their bodies, looking for the devil's mark before they were thrown into gaol. Most would be tortured to confess their joining in wedlock with the devil and only the lucky ones would be allowed to die with ease.

Poppy would wonder then at sixteen, as she wondered now at her birth, what other lives she would live. She tried to look forward further but saw only white light. Whatever lay further she could not possibly imagine yet. It lay too far away. She trusted it would be a good life next time.

*   *   *

Either the gin was stronger than Joseph realized or the heat more than he was used to, because he fell asleep. When he woke it was dark and he knew he had been dreaming about the eyes again. Those eyes had tormented him for as long as he could remember but he didn't know whose they were; only that he must fear them. When he'd planned the trip it was mainly to learn about the eyes but they didn't seem part of Old Loula story and now he was here he didn't see how they could fit in anyway.

Joseph shook away the fear and crawled out of his clothes before hanging them in the closet and slipping under the sheet for the night. He knew he should go down for a meal and then write up the notes that buzzed around his head but he did neither. He knew the manuscript needed to be rewritten. Words that had seemed okay in New York now came across as dry and lifeless.

The next morning he took the manuscript down to breakfast and flipped again through the yellowing pages of typed script. The half finished book had sat in his desk for so long yet barely a day had gone past when he hadn't considered finishing it. The truth was there were so many gaps, so much he remembered but so little he understood. Sally had died long ago, not long after they moved to New York, and as he grew up there was no one to help him make sense of the stories. He knew them as disjointed scenes, yet when he pieced them together they never went anywhere.

At last he was here, back where he was born, and speaking to the few people who might be able to help.

He looked again at the words he knew already, not noticing the breakfast or the coffee which both grew cold as he picked at them, and a part of him wanted to get into the car and drive away from it all that morning. Childish fears might be irrational but they were deeper rooted than the bone and Joseph was no longer sure he wanted to dig that far.

Finally he pushed aside the cold plate and made himself go back to see Old Loula at the spigot.

Chapter 13

Old Loula pulled at her ear then cupped her chin in her hand, delving into her memory to find the words. I have puzzled over telling this next part and don't rightly know how to do it, she said. For all Hester has tried to explain it I still don't grasp it all myself. The best I can say is she had voices she heard in her mind. The way Hester saw it she was born once before and the other life was like a story playing in her head. That gave Sissie Jane a lot of problems in that it didn't fit too good with the Bible's version of things but Libby said fair play to her if she got two bites at the cherry, especially as she didn't do too good this second time round. For my money it just seemed a little weird, being born twice, as I would hate to come across my Ma again and Aunt Violet if they was to return. It was bad enough the first time and I would not take kindly to having them back. I must confess to have gotten a little selfish with my cabin and no way would I vacate my big bed that used to be my Ma's.

The way Hester told it, and she don't speak much these days for she lives in her head mostly but I'm recalling days when she was doing her research at the library and she was young and vibrant and would sit at the spigot with us trying to convey what was going on in her mind, the way she told it was she recalled being born that other time. Fancy recalling the day you was born, and not even this life but the one before? She would tell us about the sea always being gray and stealing in, she used to say that, I recall it particular. What else now? I guess you would have to get into Hester's mind in order to understand the rest.

What was it you said your name was again, Old Loula asked of the young man listening to her tale? Joseph, he said in his gentle cultured voice. His clothes were smart and you could tell he was a professional man from the quiet way he listened. Old Loula was getting confused. She swatted at the flies, brushing them and the confusion aside. What brings you this way Mr Joseph, she asked. Research, he told her, family research.

Just then a woman shuffled out to the faucet. It was difficult to tell how old she was but she dragged her feet and her head hung over to one side.

It breaks my heart to see Hester now, said Old Loula, not dropping her voice although the woman was close enough to hear. There is a gray streak in the child's hair, just at the front and to one side, do you see? Old Loula inclined her head to where Hester was sitting herself down in the dust. Everyone says Hester is mad, she added, but I don't see how a girl of thirteen could survive any other way. I must say I blame myself and maybe Sissie and Libby for not noticing about the baby but as for the other, the incest you would call it now but we never had the fancy words back then, well how could anyone stop that when it was in most every cabin?

Joseph watched as Hester patted at the small book that poked out from the top of her dress pocket.

She always wears a dress or skirt with a pocket just right for a small book, said Old Loula, and if the dress has no pocket of its own she will stitch one on. She never takes much care selecting the material for the patch pocket and the strange way she looks and dresses only makes folk think her more touched. She will insist on wearing a print dress with a canvas pouch tacked on the front for her book. Old Hester they will call her soon, but she is not old. It is just that she is no longer young ... not that she ever was. There was a time when Hester's body was young, and small ... a raggedy little muffin she was then ... but young? Never that I truly recall.

Old Loula scratched an itch she had found on her thigh and then continued talking to Joseph. Now they calls her a child murderer, she said. A long time ago they stopped calling her the child as got born and kilt her mother and started with 'Hester, that one as kilt her own baby'. It is never enough to be known as who you are, it has to be a part of what you has done. I suppose that is the way of it.

She goes to the library each Thursday fortnight when she gets her ride into town. Of course there is just the one library for all folks now and the room downstairs is just a storeplace for old books and packing boxes, with some dusty filing parceled up in the corner. That is where Hester does her reading still. Abigail is long dead, of course, but a nice lady clerk puts out a selection of books on the wood table, just under the ceiling lamp hanging in the basement, and unlocks the door special for Hester. Jenny, I believe that is her name, the new young assistant who first took over from

Abigail. Just two books each time is all Hester will take, small ones so they can be carried to the spigot in her patch pocket. The lady clerk, Jenny, that is it I'm sure, Jenny never even bothers her for a ticket.

Joseph looked over to where Hester had settled herself on the ground. She opened a book on her lap but let the pages turn themselves idly in the slight breeze. Hester was humming a piece of tune, a field holler, quietly to herself. He called over to her, trying to introduce himself, but she never looked up and when she did finally turn her head towards him, her eyes were focused on something else. Or maybe not focused at all.

Old Loula started throwing stones at the few chickens scratching in the dirt and Joseph realized she was missing the attention. Now where were we, he said, getting out his notebook. But for all Old Loula started with the story again, her mind wandered and she just went over old ground.

After just a short time she picked up her pail and walked off, leaving Joseph alone on the seat.

Joseph looked around him but there was no one else around. A young girl had walked past earlier but she had gone now and there never seemed to be any real signs of life in the few cabins that stood in the clearing. He walked over to where Hester sat and carefully brushed aside a fly that was walking on her face. He seemed to caress her cheek but she never noticed, her hands staying clasped round the outside covers of the small book in her lap.

He remembered the child Hester and her visits to the forbidden house down by the creek. He too had voices in his head but his were more real and more recent. To this day he could hear the voice of a young girl whispering to him as he tottered on childish legs around the bruised and tearful Hester. He had waited many years to complete his own picture, to find out about the life he too carried around, second hand, in his head. And he was frightened of the eyes because a young girl had told him to be, but he didn't know whose they were. It had been difficult, carrying around a fear and not knowing what he was frightened of, just a heavy weight burning in the pit of his stomach.

He tried talking to the adult Hester again but she didn't seem to notice so he patted her on the shoulder and then went back over to the seat.

He waited some more, still not sure if Old Loula was coming back, then picked up his notebook again and drew a pen from his pocket. The words he had written ten years before were stale and meaningless, he decided, so he started afresh. This time he wanted the story to come to life, the way it had when Hester first told him.

As Joseph started to write he kept looking over to Hester but she never acknowledged he was there. Her hands stayed gripped on either side of her book and she stared hard at the pages in front of her. He couldn't be sure but Joseph didn't think she turned a page the whole time he sat there.

* * *

POPPY'S STORY BY JOSEPH G JEFFERSON. DRAFT 2. CHAPTER 1 - MANNINGTREE 1628

Page 1.

Hester fought to remember her own past. Sitting in the heat of a Southern summer, on the hard mattress of her trundle bed, she gazed across the room and out the window at the airless morning in front of her. There had been times when she felt the girl in her head was so close and she groped out now, searching for her again. Slowly it started to happen. It was like a dream, although Hester knew she was not asleep. The cold spring morning of 1628 began to intrude and Hester waited for the scene to unfold in her mind. Heliotrope, the wicce woman, took a handful of ferns and covered the serving girl's face, noticing the cold blue-white of the young skin against her own large chapped hands. Heliotrope was worried now for the child, the baby who would grow into the girl in Hester's head.

Sarah Fletcher was in the clearing when Heliotrope got back, the child wet and swaddled in petticoats. Of the two friends, Sarah was delicate and short where Heliotrope was broad shouldered, tall and heavy breasted. Both were in their middle years and had the lined faces of women who knew few comforts. Heliotrope shook her head to clear the raindrops from her eyes but her wet hair stayed glued in strips across her ample face. Sarah was a bright woman and there was no need for her to ask after Rose the serving girl. She was dead, obviously.

They both ducked under the canvas door into the hut, Sarah taking the baby and stripping off its wet wrappings while Heliotrope stepped out of her clothes and sat wrapped in a cloth waiting for them to dry.

'A girl,' Sarah said, happy. 'A baby girl.'

The child kicked now, almost energetically, despite its pale color and the chill of its skin, the little legs pummeling the cold air and the arms punching free of the sodden petticoats. In the half-light of the windowless hut neither of the women noticed the energy was not evenly divided and that for every fierce kick from the right leg there was only a half-hearted twitch from the left, countered by a small wave of the left hand.

'Just look at her,' said Sarah, 'she is beautiful. Have you seen those eyes?' She looked up to where Helly sat on the straw pallet. 'Do not worry so,' she went on hurriedly. 'We will take care of her. Look, you keep her close for warmth and I'll damp up some bread in a cloth for her to suck.'

'She be needing milk,' said Heliotrope, a deep, resonating voice in a small hut.

'That be so,' agreed Sarah. 'And I'll be the one to find it for her. But first we must get her suckling afore she forgets how. Then it's off looking for a milch cow.'

'Or a goat,' agreed Heliotrope, allowing herself to relax a little. 'Not a bad time of year to find a nanny in milk,' she said.

Sarah hunkered down, drawing her skirts around her legs and up away from the damp earth floor. This time of year it could be almost as wet inside the hut as out, if you lived too near the bog as they did. There was no drained land where the poor and the outcast lived. She bent over the clay pot where the food was stored and crumbled some bread into a strip of cloth. Then she tied the material with a knot at the top and dipped the whole into a jar of water that stood by the door. When it had absorbed plenty, she pulled aside the door flap and squeezed out the excess onto the grasses outside, fashioning a nipple-like point at the end.

'There,' she said, 'breakfast fit for a new baby girl,' and she gave it to Heliotrope to try on the child. 'It be what the women in the town use when the milk won't come,' she added.

'And the children die for lack of milk goodness,' said Heliotrope as she brushed the cloth bag over the child's lips.

'I hear what you say,' said Sarah. 'See? I am off just now.' She threw a shawl around her and picked up an empty pot from the floor before going out the sack door. 'And if it fails, we can try a breast each and see if the gods will send us any milk for our efforts and determination,' she said.

'Two childless virgin women?' queried Helly.

'Qualities worthy of extra credit so the Christian women say,' replied Sarah, making herself chuckle.

When Heliotrope was left alone with the child she tried the bread pap. She opened the tiny lips with her fingers and urged drips of the bread milk into the child's mouth. For the first time, the baby went to cry, screwing up its eyes and opening its mouth as if to yell, surprising Helly when she realized how quiet the child had been until then. But no noise came. The baby did not cry.

'Shhh baby,' she comforted, rocking her gently and taking the opportunity of an open mouth to push the food in again.

This time the child choked and she was forced to put the bag aside as she turned the baby on its side and rubbed its back while it gasped for air.

It was then that a third woman from the marshes, Meg, pushed aside the sack door and entered. It was common courtesy to call out or signal your arrival with a whistle or cough, but Meg was not one for courtesies. She was a blunt woman, a highlander, and not widely liked among the group of outcasts living by the marsh. Shunned themselves by the villagers the others found a common bond, but Meg alone was separate again, apart from the loners. It annoyed Heliotrope because she knew she should have liked the woman better. She just wasn't likable. Only Sarah found time for her.

'Rose has birthed the bairn then?' said Meg, before she was quite in the room, her eyes not yet adjusted, unable to see for herself. Her voice was high and harsh with its clipped highland accent for she had traveled further than most in her efforts to avoid persecution.

The last grayness of the day flooded bright into the dark

windowless hut, through the doorway, past the tall frame of Meg and the heavy sack she held over her head.

That was another thing that annoyed Heliotrope, when Meg confirmed, over and over, that she knew the pattern of events before she learnt of them. Heliotrope was known by all to be the wise woman and yet it was becoming more frequent for Meg to be ahead of her.

'Yes. A girl,' answered Heliotrope. 'But Rose herself is dead, may the gods protect her now.'

She spoke quickly, before Meg could say it first. That would truly make her riled, if Meg had seen Rose's death and she had not. She was finding it so difficult these days to foresee things that were close to her. It was a simple matter to sit with a stranger and feel his life flow over her, to hand out a string of knots to a sailor to protect him from the worst brushes he would have with the fates. There was no difficulty in that. Strangers merely had to sit with her and the room became filled with their lives, past and future, and she would see clearly if they might heed her advice or no. Her true art was in shutting out their lives, to keep them separate from her own, to allow in just as much as she was paid for and no more. It was her only income, the trinkets the sailors paid with, goods she could trade for corn and eggs, but she was not paid to be burdened with their lives. That was a heavy enough load she carried for her friends. She opened herself to strangers just long enough to hand out advice to those who wanted to take it, to string protective knots into a piece of twine, silk or plaited hair and instruct when each knot should be undone.

'So, the serving girl dies,' stated Meg, unsurprised. She came over to the pallet and sat herself down, taking the bundle from Heliotrope and pulling back the wrappings. 'She is nay a good'un,' she said of the child.

Heliotrope refused to move quickly, to show anxiousness, to give herself away. Calmly, she looked closely now and saw, for the first time, the difference in the two sides of the child's body. The energy on the right and the struggle on the left. It was almost a relief to find it was only a physical weakness that Meg had seen and she had stupidly overlooked. There were worse things. And a damaged body often held a perfect soul, that was well known. It was the other that Helly had feared when she first heard Meg's words, that the child was an evil soul, one of the few that managed to come back time and again, with nothing better to do with their new time on earth than to jeopardize the lives and souls of others. It was the one thing that sometimes caused Heliotrope to reflect on the Christians' belief that there was a spirit of evil, a devil. It was not something they had ever taught in their own religion. There was only the balance of good and bad, and the gods could be humored or out of humor but they were never truly evil.

'She was a long time getting born I'll warrant,' Meg said.

'She needs milk,' said Heliotrope. 'Sarah has gone looking.'

'A waste of good milk if she finds it,' said Meg.

No, Meg was wrong, thought Heliotrope as she stretched over and laid her fingers on the child's eyes, her sizable fingers resting lightly around the small skull. No picture formed in her head or presence filled the room, even though she sought it, but she found a strength there that she wanted to believe in. There was something Meg had not seen. Something Heliotrope felt keenly.

'This child must be allowed to live,' she started, 'I can see she has a great role to play.'

It was a lie. Heliotrope never lied. It was vanity. Claiming knowledge over Meg's. Heliotrope knew she had started on an unwise path, and she also knew she would follow it.

Meg snorted. 'Send her back,' she said. 'She doesn'a belong on this earth.'

'She will live and grow, and I will watch over her,' said Heliotrope.

'The child is weak already and she'll no see the week's end. Her soul was never meant to more than touch. Some of them don't. You know that, if anyone does.'

Yes, souls touching and leaving again. It was a common enough thing. Then why did the gods send her to me, thought Heliotrope, if they wanted her back? They would not send her to me if they wanted her back, surely?

'You be wrong Meg Southly,' she said. 'She has a role to play.'

'She'll sicken and die Mistress Heliotrope, and if you keep her alive against the wishes o' the gods then you are more a fool than I had believed.'

Meg wrapped the child again, against the chill of the air, and went to hand her back. She changed her mind for a moment and brought the bundle to her lips to kiss the girl on her forehead before placing her on the straw bed. Then she rose to go. All the while the child had not murmured or cried once.

'I will tell you one thing only,' Meg said. 'This child will be the death of us all.'

And with that she left.

Heliotrope waited until the sound of Meg's feet splashing in the open puddles had died away before she unwrapped the layers of cloth once again and stared down at the child. It was probably the cold rush of air that did it, but the baby's right arm closed in suddenly towards her chest, slapping against Heliotrope's own hand. The tiny fingers wrapped tight around the dangling wet strands of Heliotrope's hair and stayed clenched.

With the child pulling her hair like that it was more difficult but Heliotrope studied the small body, its one leg kicking. It was true. And what was more she should have seen it herself. The girl was weak on one side. She rubbed the still foot and leg, wondering if the affliction would keep her from walking. There was a poppy red mark on her right thigh.

'We had best find you a name,' Heliotrope said aloud, 'because I will not let you go now.'

She didn't know if it was in spite of, or because of Meg Southly that she felt this way, but she was determined the girl was going to survive. She looked again at the red mark and was pleased to see it was on the strong leg. Good, she thought. She wrapped her up tightly and left her on the bed while she tried to dress in the dry shawls and cloths that she could find, very aware that she was waiting for the baby to cry. It would be too cruel if she were dumb as well. After lighting the tallow lamp she tried again with the bread pap, but the child would only choke over it.

An hour later, when Sarah burst in through the cloth door with barely a warning, the wind from the doorway blew out the lamp. Sarah was wet and cold and without the milk.

'Needs must we leave now,' she panted. 'There be trouble at Thorn Inn.'

Sarah was breathless from running but she started collecting the things they would need, putting them on the pallet bed. Heliotrope found a cloth bundle to tie them in then wrapped the baby in sacking, hoping it would keep the rain off the child.

'They say as how the women at the bog be sheltering the Huguenots,' said Sarah now she was getting her breath back, 'and now the church people be raising up a posse to flush us all out.'

'There were accusations against us before and we weathered them,' said Heliotrope.

'But this time the parson has a knife through his eye and there is a Huguenot laid out dead in the gaol,' explained Sarah.

So religion would hound them again. Unless you could prove yourself a dedicated member of this new church then you were declared its enemy. The women's own faith never held with converting others. Anyone could join them if they so chose but they were as happy to see others following their own path. But the big stone church was now the law of the land and from what Sarah said it seemed this time would be nastier than before, with the anger against the Huguenots going against anyone they could find in the bog lands beyond Mistley Thorn. The bog wasn't a place you lived from choice. You lived there because you hid from something. To the wiccan women, who still believed in their old gods and worshipped the land itself, it seemed strange that with both factions sharing the same one god the Huguenots and the Protestants should so despise one another, religions of peace trying to kill one another to prove which was right, or stronger, or both. But there was money involved and that made it all the more dangerous. There was profit for all in denouncing your neighbor if you stood to rob his house while he was fleeing and gain his land for your own when he dare not come back. And the king took his share as a confiscature. It was a bad system that allowed theft under the banner of patriotism. But what was there to steal from the wise women?

They snatched up what they could and went out into the rain,

Heliotrope barely dried out and Sarah already soaked through from her run to the village. It was dark now but finding their way around wasn't the problem, it was knowing where to go that would be safe.

'I give her the name Poppy,' said Heliotrope. 'Poppies be brighter than Roses.'

'But be they any hardier?' Sarah wanted to know.

❀   ❀   ❀

They took a treacherous route out of the Tendring Hundred, trusting they knew it better than anyone else who might follow, and skirted a long way out from Mistley Thorn before joining the river and shadowing it up as far as Manningtree itself. Neither of them had been to the Manor before. It was the place where Rose the serving girl had worked and it was Poppy's father that owned it.

Poppy's eyes really were unusual, Sarah noticed. She shifted the child and its wrappings onto her other hip. She motioned for Heliotrope to rest awhile for her back must be breaking too for the weight of their possessions in that bundle would be considerable and they had been traveling for most of the night now. They found themselves a felled tree that was far more inviting than the rest of the mud. It was still quite dark but Sarah could see Poppy's eyes glinting up at her, inquiring, wanting to know what was going on, or so Sarah believed.

'Will you stop cooing at the thing,' cursed Heliotrope harshly under her breath. The woman was driving her mad with talking to the child. It wasn't a full day old yet and Sarah Fletcher had talked to it all the way from the marshes.

'We have to make her welcome in this world or she may decide not to stay,' said Sarah plainly.

Heliotrope sat her bulk on the felled tree, put her head in her hands and drew a slow breath.

'You know you are my friend Sarah Fletcher, but you are also a fool of a woman and you would drive the Wiccan Council to the Church of England just to escape the sound of your voice,' she said eventually.

Heliotrope was chilled through to the bone and she had sunk waist deep in the marsh bogs several times that night before they had got on firm ground again. She had insisted on going first, in the dark, to pick the safest route, with Sarah holding Poppy and following behind. Poppy. She was getting used to calling her that now, in her mind, rolling it around for practice, just in case the child should stay and grow with them. She hoped she would.

'Take my words as those of a soul fatigued and freezing to the bone,' said Heliotrope with a change of heart. 'You be a good soul Sarah Fletcher.'

'And you be chilled through Heliotrope and I had not thought it. Will you take my clothes and swap? They have only the night dew on them now, as it is long past raining. Yours have such mud on them as will never dry out.'

Heliotrope refused, for the offer was mostly a courtesy, what with Sarah being such a small thing. They were barely rested before Heliotrope was anxious to press on for Manningtree Manor. She thought the plan was a fool one but she had no other to replace it.

It was less than an hour later that they found dry scrubland and followed a path through it. Eventually it opened out and they could see Manningtree Manor rising almost in front of them. The air was still damp from the mists but it was nearly morning now, with the sky brightening blue mauve over to the east.

It seemed the serving girl Rose faded at just the right time, as far as the father of the child was concerned. He refused an audience to Heliotrope and Sarah although he did send the cook back down to check if the child might be a boy.

Sarah had persuaded Heliotrope to call at the back of the manor and not stride through the front courtyard as she intended. It got them a good meal at least and milk for Poppy because the cook took pity. The cook had never taken kindly to the way Rose caught the master's eye but that didn't get in the way of a little compassion. She said she knew it would come to this, but wasn't the little one a beauty, after all? She changed the wet cloths around the baby in a businesslike manner but chucked her under the chin before handing her back to Sarah. The master wouldn't acknowledge a bastard daughter and that was that, said the cook, and a fool Rose was for thinking otherwise. But it was a shame Rose was dead, when all was said and done, and things might have been different if it had been a boy. The master and his lady were getting desperate for an heir and there was talk lately of taking in a nephew, Nathaniel, to raise as their own. The cook didn't like the boy and she made no effort to hide it.

The cook gave them hot food while their clothes dried by the fire and even warmed the milk by plunging in a hot poker, but that was the only visit Poppy was ever to make to Manningtree Manor.

Heliotrope and Sarah would keep moving over the next few months, hearing of trouble before it came to the door and pressing on to a new camp to stay always one step ahead. After a time life in the marshes of Tendring Hundred would return to as near normal as it ever could be and they would go back to their home to raise the child Poppy with the other outcasts.

✿   ✿   ✿

Sitting on her trundle bed in the small cabin, Hester felt the heat of the day invade her thoughts and nearly lost the images in her head. She slapped at a mosquito on her arm and the hot dry dust parched her throat before she sunk again into the story. For a moment the two worlds merged and she felt them both in tandem. Her ears relayed the barking of a dog in the yard and the crowing of a cock as it scratched in the heat at the faucet. Yet her small white, child's feet were being set down on the cold stone flags of the church porch and the coolness of the memory dragged her back to the other world. Heliotrope, Poppy's Yarb Mother, had carried her as far as the church where she put her down on the stone floor and told her she was a big girl now. Four years was old enough to walk yourself to church, she said.

By the time the child Poppy was four the women of the marshes found themselves left in peace for six days out of every seven. In exchange for their attendance at church each Sunday, now a law of the land, they were allowed an uneasy freedom.

120

'Be it Sunday today?' Poppy asked, looking past the heavy studded door and into the emptiness of the stone building beyond.

'There be something important that I need show you Poppy,' said Heliotrope as she pushed the wooden door further open, although she made no move to go inside. Poppy could see now, there was no one else in the church.

'Be the others coming?' Poppy wanted to know. She didn't mean the churchgoers, she meant their friends, Sarah Fletcher, Rose Hallybread, Martha, and Elizabeth and Rebecca. Poppy was young but she knew her friends went to church each Sunday because it was the law, but there were others they called the churchgoers because they chose to go. If Poppy, Heliotrope and Sarah missed a Sunday without good reason they would be put in the gaol, Poppy told herself, remembering Heliotrope's words as religiously as the parson's. Everyone had to go to church on Sunday, she knew that, but they did their worship at home, together. When they came to the church on Sundays they kept their our own thoughts in their heads, to widen those of the parson. Heliotrope had told her that. And Sarah Fletcher had added how his prayers were too narrow and selfish, and he would forget to ask his people to pray for the earth while they were so busy caring about themselves. Poppy knew she and the others must look after the earth first, and the plants and animals, and only then could they worry about people. Or else the earth would die. That is what they prayed for when the parson said the prayers for his own soul.

'Be the others coming?' repeated Poppy when the only answer she had got was a smile and a pat on the head. She fidgeted her smaller foot until it was tucked behind her other leg and mostly hidden by her skirt. It was a habit she was getting into.

'I have a lesson to teach you Poppy, but our friends know it already,' Heliotrope told her, 'and today is not Sunday but Woden's day, as you should know.'

They stayed silently at the entrance to the church, Poppy trying to keep her foot still under her guardian's gaze, until Heliotrope asked quietly, 'Do you know where this church be built?' The tone of her voice made Poppy see the seriousness of the question. 'Feel it,' Heliotrope continued, 'close your eyes and feel where we be.'

Poppy did as she was asked but she didn't know what answer was expected from her. All she could feel was that the place was old. The oldness and the chill of the stones swarmed round her, chanting a wind song she could barely hear. Pictures formed in her head of large stones ringed in a circle. She could see men smashing the big stones into smaller chunks for building, thinking to shatter the circle's power at the same time, but she was shy of saying to Heliotrope what came into her head, that the church was made from some of the circle stones.

'No,' she said at last, worried that her answer, if she told it, would be a foolish one and childish.

Heliotrope squatted down so her eyes were level with Poppy's own and took both small hands in her great fingers to hold them against the gray stones of the church porch. Then she told Poppy the story of the church.

'Some blame Pope Gregory,' she explained, 'but I do not care to lay blame. This church was built on the site of an old temple, as were most churches. They strove to convert all the people to the new religion, to stamp out the old ways,' she said, taking Poppy by the hand now and leading her inside the church, lifting her so she could place her hands on the stone walls. 'Feel that,' she told her. 'Do you feel the warmth of many people through the cold of the stone? The warmth of 25,000 years, for that is how long we have worshipped the earth and her stones. This new way we are forced to learn is a young religion and Pope Gregory thought he might convert us all by building his churches over the old temples, by smashing idols and sprinkling holy water. What he did not think to control were the artisans and craftsmen who did his dirty work for him. For it was their religion too he was destroying and they wove their own old deities into the new churches. If they were to be forced to his new church every Sunday then they would have their own worship at the same time. Look, over there,' she said, putting the child down and pointing her to face the door. 'Who do you see?' she asked her.

The stone woman above the door was round, and ugly. She had an open mouth and a fat belly with her legs flung apart. Poppy had never noticed her there before, carved small in the stone over the door. She was not like the figures at the altar.

'This is Shiela-na-gigs, our fertility mother,' explained Heliotrope. 'And who is this?' she asked, pointing to a stone man wreathed in leaves and creepers that grew from his head and ears and almost covered him. It was a small figure at the head of a pillar. Small but with life. 'Who do you think it might be?' she asked Poppy.

The child was still nervous of giving the wrong answer.

'Is he our Robin of the Woods?' she said at last.

'Yes. Our Jack of the Green. Our forest man,' said Heliotrope, laughing as she looked at him, then holding the child high so she could stretch out her hand but she could not possibly reach him. 'They may have roofed this place in stone and plaster,' said Heliotrope, 'but still the woodsman comes in to see us. When they built this church, the artisans and stonemasons wanted to bring nature inside. If they must worship indoors, then they must bring a part of their green under the roof, that was their reasoning.'

It was then that Heliotrope walked her to the quiet carvings at the front of the church, the ones with sad faces. Poppy knew these figures because she listened hard to her lessons on Sundays. Heliotrope pointed to the images of God and Mary and Jesus. When she gave them their real names of Osiris, Isis and Horus they were not strange to Poppy for these were the gods they had at home. Poppy looked into the face of Isis, or Mary, wondering what had made her so sad.

'And Jesus was born on Christmas Day,' repeated Poppy.

Heliotrope patted her head again before she told her how the Christian religion had needed to be bent before it would be accepted, that the old worshippers had always celebrated that time of year, that Christmas was really the Feast of the Winter Solstice. She said Pope Gregory's men let the people keep their feast days but put Christianity into them. That if they had not, the folk would never have agreed and become churchgoers. Some of us still do not agree, she said.

Heliotrope took Poppy's hand, the small one that she said was her favorite because she could pour more love into the small one and it would never be full, and walked the child around the great pillars of the church. She was silent for so long Poppy wondered if she had been forgotten. Eventually, Heliotrope hunkered down and took Poppy's chin in her hand. She smiled.

'And do you know why this Pope Gregory felt compelled to stamp out all that went before?' asked Heliotrope, talking softly so Poppy knew it was important, 'to destroy it one way or another with his own ideas, not content to let the prayers of all live in harmony beside each other? For surely, we never mind if another thinks differently from ourselves, do we, unless it is evil thoughts?' she qualified.

Poppy did not understand so she said nothing.

'Because of women,' Heliotrope said in a whisper. 'The old ways looked to us women, our knowledge and inheritance handed down from mother to daughter, women guarding the religion. And that power frightens the men that hold the new religion. They are afraid of us Poppy,' she said. 'They will be afraid of you when I teach you all I know.'

They left the church then, the woman and the child, going out into the bright sun with the grass soft and giving under their feet after the cold stone slabs.

'I like it out here,' said Poppy. 'Is this where the old temple was? Outside? Under the sun and the stars?'

'Yes,' said Heliotrope, and pulled the child towards her warm, ample thigh where she patted her head and the girl smelled the sweetness of her.

❖   ❖   ❖

Hester didn't know what hit her but one moment she was watching a story unfold in her head and the next she was halfway across the bedroom floor and piling hard into the frame of Solomon's bed. Her ear rang and she put up her hands to catch the next blow, but it never came. By the time she focused, her father was striding back through the kitchen and across to the porch door. She tried calling out to him but he took no notice and she watched him from the window as he walked away. She supposed it must be time for lunch but she had been lost in her thoughts since clearing away the breakfast dishes.

Hester went to the pantry shelf and took down the vegetables that needed preparing. She had meant to get everything on to boil before she indulged once more in the story of Poppy but she found herself drifting back, easy as anything, with the paring knife in her hand and the greens in front of her. It was like sinking into a good book.

Helly was Poppy's Yarb Mother. She never minded if the child called her Helly, or Heliotrope. She always called her Mother if the others were listening, for a child of six must not be disrespectful of its elders.

'Mother,' she called, for Sarah Fletcher was with them today. 'Mother,' she said, 'may I fetch the yarbs for Mistress Fletcher.'

They laughed, both Heliotrope and Sarah Fletcher, thinking a young girl with a crippled foot could never tell tongue of dog and adder's fork from other plants growing in the woods and meadows. Well, Poppy could tell her yarbs and she wanted to show them. But they scorned her in the kindest way, stroking her yellow hair and pulling at her pouting lower lip with their fingers to make her stop.

'It's Paul Podgam we be needing today,' Heliotrope said.

'I can find him,' Poppy told them, dancing away on her strong right foot and catching up the yarb basket from where it stood at the door of their house, leading the way.

They called it a house but really it wasn't. The bones of it were woven in sticks to the shape of a hut and a solid covering of mud, horse hair and dung cement kept out the rain. There was a doorway, but no door to speak of, just a cloth pinned against the entrance. It did its best to keep out the cold in bad weather but it could never stop the creeping sea mist. Besides, from the inside it was only the flapping of the sacking against the doorway that gave them light. Where would they be for light if there were a real wood door to close them in with? No, the sack door was fine for them.

'Wait for us Poppy,' the two women said, but the child picked up the basket and ran on without them. It was her game to reach the copse before them. The copse lay beyond the meadow. The girl with her small child's legs, and one smaller again and dragging, tried to outrun the two women with their straight, strong limbs. But she would beat them. It was important to her.

She broke into a run, the warmth of her breath showing clouds of white on the cold morning. There was no trouble with her leg. Waiting for her slow leg was like waiting on an old friend. You knew they wouldn't let you down. It was the stitch in her side that hurt and made her stop before she even saw the river. She had run too fast and breathed too shallow, and the basket was nearly as big as she was. She was tired of being so small. It was tedious, waiting to grow, but somewhere in her head, she thought she had done this before. But the more she thought it the less she remembered these days.

'Have you found it yet, young Poppy?'

It was Heliotrope, taunting her. She knew she was not there yet, in the copse where the best Paul Podgam grew. Poppy would not be made a fool of for all her Yarb Mother was dear to her, so she set to looking. On the path where Poppy stood there would be no Paul Podgam, and if there was it would be small and useless, but she looked all the same. It was important that she prove her knowledge of the yarbs. Important to her.

She searched through the wet leaves, barely stopping to say good day to a fine lady spider that was weaving her dewy cobweb home between two frail stalks of grass. Yet she couldn't quite pass her by without a small acknowledgment. Poppy did so love spiders, and it saddened her that she must eat them wrapped in their houses to keep Old Johnny, the ague, away. But they were her friends all the same, even when she ate them wrapped as pills, for they kept her safe. Good morrow Mistress Spider. How are you this wet grass spring morning? Well, I hope? And so too am I, you will be pleased to hear, and not needing of yourself and home to keep Old Johnny from me. Weave away, Mistress Spider, it is springtime now, and past the season of Old Johnny's mischief.

She blew a kiss to the spider and passed on as swift as she could in search of Paul Podgam, brushing the wet leaves and stalks with the palm of her right hand, parting the grass from the yarbs.

'Poppy?'

That was Heliotrope's voice. She was concerned now, because Poppy hid in the shadow from the hedges and she thought she had lost her charge.

The basket was too heavy, the course willow sticks woven so tightly and the handle so dense and weighted, and Poppy could carry it no further. So she placed it against a trustworthy tree and crept along free. No basket.

'Poppy? You will never find Paul Podgam here my dear. He grows in quite a different place from this.'

Now it was Sarah speaking. Funny then, how she said the words just as Poppy's fingers clenched around the stem of polypodium fern. And it was a fine fellow, this Paul, growing strong in the shade of a beech tree.

The stem was as stubborn as Poppy and that was how Heliotrope found them, battling together. The grooves in Poppy's clenched hand were all bloodied with trying, and Paul Podgam's stem was all spent and broken but still hanging on with a thread or two.

'Look at your hand, child,' scolded Sarah.

'And a fine yarb specimen too,' confirmed Heliotrope, 'for all that he is growing here in the meadow and not down in the copse where he should be. A fine Paul Podgam.'

'Polypodium,' said Poppy.

They both looked at her then.

'What did you call it?' Heliotrope asked Poppy.

'Polypodium,' she told her again. 'Polypodium fern.'

'Now there be a funny name,' she said.

'That be its real name,' Poppy heard herself saying.

'Well,' said Heliotrope slowly, 'then I shall believe you.'

And that was all. An end to it. Heliotrope cut the reluctant stem strings with a knife she kept on her always, and carried away the polypodium as gently as any baby. She found the basket easily. She placed the one in the other and all three headed for home. What pleased Poppy most was knowing her polypodium was quality enough. If Heliotrope had questioned its value to the remedy, she would have continued to the copse for more. So Poppy was pleased with herself and her yarb, but she longed to be bigger than six.

* * *

Hester was still sitting in the dust less than ten feet away when Joseph stopped writing. He asked her if she wanted to see the words in his notebook but she never looked up. He started to pack away his things, telling her he would be back the next day, explaining how he had booked just a few days away from work and the time was running out. She never stirred so he walked over to her and patted the top of her head the way she had patted his own so long ago. He had loved that. It had made everything better again.

Chapter 14

Old Loula was waiting at the faucet next morning when Joseph arrived. Hester was sitting on the bench beside her so Joseph spread his cotton jacket on the ground and sat down to face them.

It was later than usual because Joseph had been into town, looking for a store that could print out from the computer file he'd saved. He had spent the evening cutting huge sections from his manuscript and retyping fresh new passages. It wasn't easy but at least now he had an idea of what he wanted to do. The story of Poppy was far more than a remembered history. Times told to him by a tearful young girl when he was too young to accept the words or their meaning.

Joseph had been up much of the night so he was tired. He said good morning to both women but neither responded and he felt his heart sink. Once again he wondered what in hell he was doing there but he pulled his notebook from the jacket pocket anyway, wanting to check the things he had intended to ask. He had barely opened his mouth to speak when Old Loula started up with her story as if nothing had happened the day before.

Now I recall that time like it was yesterday, she said taking out a faded handkerchief from her sleeve and mopping at the sweat on her cheeks, though Lord knows how many years back we are talking, she added. Young Hester was that excited you would of thought she had met this girl Poppy herself and found a friend. To tell the truth of it, there was some as thought she plum made it up, the whole story, like those kids as has friends they imagine and talks to even when they ain't there. Of course I never doubted Hester's telling of it, then or now, but I was mindful to play skeptical on account of enough folk found me weird without courting trouble.

Anyhow, that day Hester come skipping up, right up to my cabin, never waiting until I was ready to visit the spigot again before supper. It was some time after lunch though Hester said as how Solomon had got the hump and wandered off without eating. That girl was so confused at that time I swear she never knew what it was Solomon wanted of her. She tried pleasing him but, what with the book reading and her mind wandering, she was in trouble most times like as not.

I still have not told you much about that girl Poppy from long ago, have I? Well, Hester ran up to mention about the girl in her head and how she could see her visiting the church and plucking herbs and all. I listened and soon learned a whole lot more. It was like Hester could dip into her head and pull out another piece of story so she give me the benefit of how it worked. I was sat on my rocker and Hester curled up on the floor beside me. She did not look at me and I went straight on pretending as how I was not listening. It was just a thing we had between us. Hester understood. It was then it started. I have since been to the movie theater and I would say it was like that only I could not see the pictures, but Hester told me of them. Maybe it was more like the radio, I don't know. And they talked funny, saying things like he *be* doing such and such, not he *is* doing it. See the funny way of talking? But I do recall it, even now, and I believe I can give a fair account of it if I try.

'Helly, he be coming,' said Hester, telling me the words Poppy was saying as she watched the story in her head. Helly was short for Heliotrope she told me, and that was the Herb Mother woman.

'Who child?' Heliotrope asked her. 'Who be coming?'

Poppy was after getting her breath back now. 'The Witchunter,' she said, with an eye to Heliotrope's face.

'In Mistley is he?' Heliotrope wanted to know.

'Not yet,' said Poppy, thinking about her answer and trying to feel was it close or not. Heliotrope trusted Poppy's sight more than her own those days, see? But she never would say so. She was the wise woman after all. Poppy would of been about thirteen years old at that time. She listened to the voices in her mind and rattled them off like she could see the Whitchunter's list. But she caught herself just before one of the names was out. It was Sarah Fletcher's, their friend.

Helly wanted to know was Poppy seeing time or distance when she said the Witchunter was near and Poppy said she would be taller, so that kind of answered that. The important thing is she could see the trouble was coming.

* * *

The perspiration was beading on Old Loula's face again. It was hot under the sun as she took out her handkerchief a second time and mopped her old wrinkled face. I won't never forget that day, she said, on account of the odd thing Hester said.

'Don't you see Miss Loula?' she asked me then, jumping up from the cabin floor and all but pitching into the rocker alongside of me. 'Don't you see it?' she said. 'Poppy is just like me. She can see things before they happen too.'

Little Hester was that excited. It's like this is the first time she has found any person to understand her and her strange way of seeing backwards and forwards in time. Now I may not be the brightest woman, said Old Loula, but even I could see as how Poppy was not real in a flesh and blood kind of way. It was no wonder Hester finally found someone to see things her way when she imagined the girl herself. Not that I told her this, of course. I am not the mean old woman Sissie Jane says I is.

So you see, I consider I understand that young Hester better than other folks for all I kept mighty quiet at the time. The stories unfolded themselves to Hester and she was apt to pass them on. For she got no judgment from my lips, one way or another, and I like to think she saw this as a safe thing she could be certain of. Looking back now I see it as a might odd, her telling stories to the wall or the sky and me pretending not to be paying no mind, but at the time we was both happy enough with the arrangement. Funny, ain't it, said Old Loula, and with that she picked up her pail of water that was now warm from the sun and shuffled slowly away in the direction of her cabin.

Hester was left sitting on the bench, her book open in front of her as usual. Joseph tried talking to her, then walked over and sat beside her, but she never looked up.

Finally he thought of an idea. He walked back to the car where he had left the leather case and returned with the newly printed pages in their plastic sleeve. He leafed through until he found the page he wanted. **Page twenty-three,** he said self-consciously, and then he coughed and wiped his mouth with a clean handkerchief. Then he read quietly to her, in a whisper, almost talking to himself. Hester never turned her head or blinked.

Hester had tried to explain the stories that played in her head,

he read, but no one else could understand. For herself, she felt the texture of the life and it was getting easier to sink into the other time, to feel herself as Poppy. The way in, she discovered, was to start a dialogue, to ask Poppy a question. Along with the answer came new sights and smells until Hester finally found herself in another body. What was the war like, Hester asked her own memories? Tell me.

Joseph looked up, not wishing to break the spell but wanting to see Hester's face. It was still as blank as before.

The civil war, whispered a small voice in her head, meant those on each side accused the other of witchcraft. It was the only way to be sure of winning. Everyone was your enemy when you could be accused for a witch. It was a strange time, full of angers and frustrations, and the church ruled the lives of all. Heliotrope said it was no wonder people were on edge, with sex proclaimed illegal, even between married couples, on Wednesdays, Fridays and Sundays, also the forty days before both Christmas and Easter, for the three days before communion and from conception to forty days after the birth of a child. That only left eight or nine weeks out of fifty-two, and taking enjoyment from an act of procreation was itself a sin. Heliotrope said it was a poor state of affairs when a religion oppressed its people so. This god of love seemed to prefer misery. The Puritans claimed poverty as a sin against God and forbade the giving of alms and bread to the poor. Times were lean and Heliotrope had to work hard to get us the lamp oil needed for the winter months. She was sitting at the quay just across from the Thorn Inn and was selling knots in a chord to one of the sailors. Tabby sat at her feet, as she often did, and Poppy, now a young woman of fifteen, dangled her feet in the water for all it was a chill afternoon and the wind was blowing up the estuary. She felt no cold because she was in love. Her Tom was a hard working farm boy, but no young man was safe from being conscripted into the army and transported halfway across the country to fight in a war that would benefit none of the poor no matter who won it. Nathaniel, as the adopted son and heir to Manningtree Manor, was the only one who felt himself safe. Heliotrope said Nathaniel was Poppy's very own cousin, but he was an arrogant man and he frightened her. There had been many times when he had asked her into the darkness of a barn but she had always escaped him.

'That be three knots,' said Heliotrope to the sailor. 'Undo the first and a breeze will blow up to guide your ship. The second will blow stronger; if you need the wind then just loosen the knot. Leave the third knot unless you have need of its power which is a gale.'

She handed over the chord and took payment of a flask of oil that the sailor had promised. She knew he was off to Great Yarmouth and on to Kings Lynn but she also felt her safeguard of knots would not be enough to protect him. Danger was written on his left palm, which showed clear now as he held out the oil. She asked to see his right hand and he held it out for her. The left was potential, the right what you made of it.

It was then that a young boy scampered past Heliotrope and threw a stick at Poppy's cat that quickly arched her back and hissed. Some were already claiming the cat to be Heliotrope's familiar so when Tabby did this everyone looked over. Suddenly the many noises of the wharf stopped.

There was a cry from a sailor sitting outside the Thorn Inn behind them. 'It's a curse she be putting on that unsuspecting man. See those knots? A curse to sink us all at sea I tell you.'

'Hush,' said another, 'think what it is you be saying.'

'Don't sail with your ship,' Heliotrope whispered to the sailor whose right hand she still held in her own. It was plain to her and also to Poppy, even though she sat a long way from him, that the ship would be lost and they could ill afford to be linked with it.

'I have no choice' tried the sailor, 'we...'

'You have the choice to live or to die and that is all I will say,' said Heliotrope as she picked up her oil and walked quickly away from the quay, signing for Poppy to follow.

Poppy said she would wait a while at Mistley, sitting beside the round pond, watching the estuary, to see if her Tom might return before nightfall. Heliotrope left reluctantly, bidding Poppy come home early, but she sat for hours before leaving her favorite tree just to the right of the inn where the mistletoe grew, and setting off for home through the woods behind the town.

Nathaniel, Poppy's cousin, surprised her, catching her and pulling her into the darkness where no one could see or hear. The warmth of his lips surprised her. The night was so cold and yet he was so warm. Surely the night was her friend, she thought, and should be the warmer of the two. It worried Poppy that Nathaniel breathed such warmth over and into her. She would be happier if he were as cold as she knew his heart to be. At least his fingers were cold, clamped around her jaw like that. Then she felt the other hand on her, gentle and stroking at her waist, easing the cloth away from her skin. How Poppy wished she were safe home early, as Heliotrope had bid her be.

The tree caught her in the back as she stepped away from him; a twig broke crisp in the cold behind her as she stumbled on the tree's roots. Don't make me fall, she asked of the tree, for you are my friend too. Nathaniel caught her, hard now, and pushed her against the tree trunk.

She felt him lifting her skirts with his free hand, the other still locked tight on her face and neck, his fingers pressed hard to the bone of her jaw as he used it to move her where he wanted. He wedged his foot between her own, then his thigh pushed into the space between and he leaned his body against her. He was angry.

'You just keep turned that way,' he told her, twisting Poppy's face to the left and expecting the one side of her to follow, for all that she was unable to move between the weight of him and the solidness of the tree. 'I don't need to see your eyes,' he spat, 'look somewhere else'.

His breath showed on the mist, moist clouds of it escaping from inside him. Quick at first, in puffs, then slower, easing out, whispering from his lips in a sneer. It smelled too, and that reassured her that she understood the world again, for good things smelled sweet and there was sour stale beer on his breath.

'Pretty from this side,' he said, looking at the right profile of her face. And it was a silly thing to say, thought Poppy, for her face was even and never was afflicted.

'Pretty,' he repeated.

Then he spat, a part of his breath forming and hanging in the air.

His fingers dug harder into her throat, his thumb pressing under her jaw, his fingers across her mouth, and he turned her head to the other side, to check.

'Pretty from this side too,' he said.

His other hand left off from under her skirts and pulled again at her smock, first drawing it free from the waist and then unlacing it at the front.

'Are these the same size then?' he sneered. 'I've always wondered.'

Of course they were the same, thought Poppy, but she wouldn't tell him. She would not speak to him. She knew he would look anyway. He was looking already. And feeling. And hurting. It was dark, and Poppy had always loved the dark. Funny how the vapor breath hung, she thought, and you could see it when so much else was obscured by black. A white fog. She wished she could see the trees more clearly. There were trees all around but it was quite dark.

His beer lips were down her neck now. Moving warm. Moving down. She tried to think of other things, of Heliotrope, of how the body was only the house for the soul. How the body was dispensable and irrelevant. But it was still her soul he was touching and she didn't like it. Try as she might Poppy could not free her soul from her body. Much as she wanted to, it made her stay. It made her feel him, tearing at the layers of clothing, stripping bare to her soul. How she wanted to step outside of herself just then.

'Lie down,' he said, pulling at her arm and scraping her back against the tree.

He was breathless now.

I will not even deign to talk to him, she thought. I can retain that much of myself.

'Bitch,' he cursed, and knocked her down.

She could feel the blood running from her nose as her back grew cold from the wet leaves.

She was afraid because this was the part she wished to save for her love Tom, but now it seemed impossible to get away from Nathaniel. She was unsure what he would do, but she believed this should be something beautiful, a gift for Tom, and she knew also that Nathaniel would prefer to steal it away.

Nathaniel dropped to his knees beside her and she could smell the strong tannin leather of his jerkin, for his clothes were fine and new. He clawed at her skirt and petticoats again. The moon came out from the clouds and she could now see his face. Again he parted her legs with his own. He grabbed beneath her, pushing her buttocks in the air with his free hand and pulled her skirt up to her chin. She knew he was staring at the red birthmark on her thigh.

'The devil's mark,' he said, 'the Witchunter will be interested to know of this if I have cause to tell him.'

'No,' she shouted at last, deciding now she would try to fight him, but he covered her mouth with his hand to silence her.

'But yes, my Poppy,' he whispered.

He pinned her to the ground with his weight and she felt something hard. He pressed against her like a tree branch and her mind raced to piece together the puzzle of his intentions. It was then he unfastened his breeches and she understood the limitations of her imagination.

'Surprised?' he asked, changing his grip on her jaw and twisting her face so she was forced to look at him.

She would not answer.

'Might it be true, then,' he said, 'that I've snared myself the last virgin in the county? That would indeed be a cure for my pox.'

Poppy tried to scream again but he put a finger to his own lips and repeated the threat to her. He had the power, he told her, to have her hung as a witch if she refused him.

Then she was angry too. She bit at Nathaniel's fingers and screamed whenever his grip lessened. Biting and screaming and not listening to Nathaniel telling her she must do as he said to save her life. Poppy screamed for anyone who might save her body.

It was a blackamoor who heard her, a storyteller from over the water he told her later when he had bloodied Nathaniel's nose for him and taken her safely back to her Yarb Mother. He was a man she would remember all her life. In fact, she thought perhaps she remembered him from before, although she couldn't be sure of when exactly. She wished she had thought to ask his name.

* * *

The sun was strong overhead and Joseph knew it was past lunch. He had some food in the car that he'd picked up from the store in town that morning. He asked Hester to wait for him and walked back to the car. He had parked under a tree but the shade had moved on and the trunk was in full sun now. He rummaged through the warm paper sacks and found some potato salad that might still be edible. The bread was okay, but moisture beads had formed inside the plastic wrapper. The ham was sealed in an airtight pack but he didn't want to take the risk. There was beer that he would have considered drinking even at that temperature if he hadn't felt it was impolite to produce alcohol in front of Hester at that time of day. It was okay in New York but people were different here in the South. He wished he had bought juice or soda. Joseph went back to the seat and laid the food on the wooden slats between them. He started eating and Hester too pulled at pieces of the bread and dipped them in the warm mayonnaise before putting them discreetly in her mouth. He said nothing but picked up the manuscript in his free hand and continued reading.

Nathaniel, her cousin, was off to accuse her of witchcraft now, he read, his voice as hushed as he felt it should be. It was this woman's memories he was voicing. **First he intended it as a blackmail threat, he continued, but then it became real for he felt forced to save himself from the shame that a cripple girl rebuffed him. If even a poor girl from the marshes rejected him then Nathaniel could not rightly call himself a man. And others would readily accept Poppy for a witch because she was born to a dead woman, born a bastard because her mother was unmarried, because she was different and the wicce woman took an interest in her, raising Poppy as her own. Because a scarlet patch of skin marked her out as their devil's own.**

Chapter 15

It was quite early when Joseph arrived back at the hotel. He went straight to his room and set up the laptop ready to write. His mind was jangling with the feeling that Hester had listened to his story. He started a fresh chapter and tried to focus, but the closeness of the meeting at the faucet had brought with it some fears too. Him whispering stories to Hester was like, was like ... with his head in his hands and his fingers massaging his eyeballs he concentrated until he saw the scrubbed wood floor of the old cabin down by the creek, for Sally had been a proud woman and the house had always been spotless, and he pictured his own chubby legs on the green fringed kitchen rug. He willed himself to open the images he had avoided over years of long dark sleepless nights. Nothing.

He got up, walked around the bed and went into the bathroom for a tumbler. Then he went into the corridor and came back with a tub of ice that he set down on the bedside table. Next he poured himself a decent sized drink, better than the mini bar, he thought. He had stopped at the store on the drive back and bought a full bottle of whiskey and some cans of soda. He knew he was on dangerous ground if he started to drink, but it was tempting all the same.

He looked at the laptop but then thought to enjoy the drink first, in peace. He closed his eyes and for a moment asked the nightmare to stay away.

*   *   *

The next morning Joseph arrived at the seat as before but Old Loula was there first. There were no more freshly printed pages. After two large tumblers of whiskey he had tried to write but the task had seemed too big, too difficult.

Joseph brought with him a folding stool he had bought at the store. It was next to the fishing rods he had stood in front of so long before deciding not to waste his time and money, but he had bought the seat with its green and white stripe canvas. He sat on it now, opposite Old Loula, leaving a space on the bench in case Hester came out. Joseph was still getting himself settled and rummaging in his pockets for a painkiller to help his head when Hester, her graying hair wrapped in a cotton headscarf, walked slowly into the clearing and took her seat. She acknowledged neither of them. Old Loula looked at her and shook her head sadly before speaking.

Now where was I, she said quietly. Oh yes, I recall. Now them times of Hester sitting up beside me and sharing her stories was not to last long, poor child. Hardly had they started it seem when she began to withdraw. That was about the time her body began to develop and not a one of us spotted the most obvious of things.

To this day I do not recall how we could of missed all the signs, for now it seems we all must of been ignoring the girl not to have noticed. She was such a skinny drip of a child that when at last her body did decide to develop itself it seem the two things got confused and those great breasts popping out like that all of a sudden just overshadowed most everything else. She was a girl of thirteen, I recall, and she did fill out in the hips too but I really think I am correct in saying she never carried any of the weight at the front like most women. She certainly never looked like she was expecting.

Sissie Jane was the only one as suspected. But for some reason Sally never did. Maybe she was wrapped up in raising her son, little Joseph, and had stopped looking out for such things. Anyhow, Sissie Jane asked a few pointed questions about Solomon but was reassured when Hester insisted everything was fine. There was certainly less bruises on her them days which led Sissie Jane to think he left her alone now but it was really that Hester just let him get on with it. If Solomon took her when he wanted then it didn't build up inside him so much. There seemed no need to take the strap to the child's legs just for the thrill of seeing her thighs, when he could strip her of her dress and drawers and take her as it pleased him. Just once her being so passive sparked his temper again and he bent her over the iron rail at the foot of the bed and took his belt to her rear end. It made him feel better when she cried out. At last she had tried to move away from him and he had to tie her again, like that first time, and it was better for him. He didn't want a ghost for a bedmate, he wanted something alive. What he wanted was his wife, but he knew she wasn't coming back.

Not long after that time when he tied her to the bed rail, Hester knew the baby was there, growing inside of her, and she could see its eyes burning as bright as her father's when he reached for the strap. That's why she knew to kill it, to stop it coming into the world and destroying ... what would it destroy? She wasn't sure, but the wickedness of the growth inside her was very clear. The unborn eyes were strong now, and ready for action. She didn't know how she knew this, but there were so many strange things she knew without learning that she just took it for the truth.

Suddenly Joseph was finding Old Loula's story difficult to take in. Finally she was touching on things he had come to find out and yet the words raced across his brain without telling him what they meant. They had turned into sounds, nothing more, a language he didn't understand. From the moment Old Loula mentioned the eyes he had gone rigid, the old cold fears creeping over him like a shadow out there in the hot sun. He tried to focus as she kept talking but he didn't know if any of it was making sense.

Many parts of the puzzle had no answer, he heard Old Loula say, but Hester knew one thing with a great certainty; this was her only moment of power against what grew inside of her.

It was a long time before Joseph's thoughts cleared enough for him to notice the story was still being told. Maybe a minute, maybe ten went by, and finally he heard Old Loula's words again, weighted by the lead that stayed in his stomach. He looked over to where Hester sat but, like always, she never showed any sign she was listening. He tried to concentrate on Old Loula's voice.

Hester went down to the crick late one afternoon, he heard her say, when the sun was laboring back down the sky. She performed each part of the ritual just as the voice in her head told her. First she stripped off her clothes, piling the cotton shift and her folded drawers beneath a bush. She had brung the hard square block of lye soap with her and a stiff brush she generally used to clean the collars of Solomon's shirts. Solomon wore Joe's shirts now and it grieved her to scrub Solomon's old man sweat off her handsome brother's Sunday best collar. Joe had bought the shirt those first weeks he worked for Mr Clarkson and Solomon had gone near crazy to find Joe's wages minus the cost of a fine shirt.

Hester climbed down the mud bank and slithered into the cool water, holding the soap and brush above her head until she was sure of her footing. Then she wet them and dug the hard bristles into the soap block as she started working up a lather. She scrubbed as the voices told her, all over, everywhere he had touched, finally parting her legs and soaping and brushing until the skin down there was raw. She had to remove all trace of Solomon and then the baby would be gone. A voice in her head told her this was true.

Finally she looked up to see the scummy bubbles drifting way downstream. The sun was almost down to the fields now. She thought it was enough. There was one last thing she could do, to be certain. She must drink gin, it was something she heard the village girls say when they was in trouble.

She waded, tired and sore, out the water and dressed herself. It all took so long, like she was drunk already. It would be dark before she got back to the cabin if she didn't hurry. And she must get back and start supper or Solomon would get angry.

She knew where to find the gin. Solomon made it himself in the lean-to beside the outhouse. She went to the cabin first and put the beans to boil, stowing the lye soap and the brush back in the tin pail where she kept them, then went looking for gin in the back. She was sore now and it hurt her more to go back down the wood steps from the porch than it had to climb them.

No one said how much gin you had to take when she had listened to the village girls discussing their own and their mother's unwanted babies but she reckoned a bottle would clean the baby out from where it sat inside of her.

The beans were burnt dry when Solomon came home. He cleared the cabin of the foul smelling smoke and set out to look for her. Libby reckoned it was lucky for Hester she found her first, because Solomon was raving by then. Libby took the girl back to her own cabin and sent Solomon home to look after hisself. She nursed Hester the next day as well, for the child was in no state to stand up. Libby put the weakness down to the corn gin but she never saw the raw, oozing skin between Hester's legs.

There must have been some small part of Hester's brain that knew the baby was still alive, but it never told the rest of her. Denial they would call it now. I have been told that. Hester plain decided it was dead and either it didn't move as it grew or she never acknowledged it moving. She blinded herself to the blazing eyes and made herself understand they were gone. That's why she didn't believe the eyelids would ever open when it was born four months later. She told herself it just took that long to abort. She was still convinced it was dead. We should call it he, because it was a boy. In her own mind it had been dead a long time.

The pains started one afternoon and Hester thought it was backache. Maybe the gas she had that morning was all a part of it. But it was after lunch she felt the pain. As she cleared away the two plates, hers and Solomon's, and the lovely black bean pot she just knew was her mother's favorite pan ... how did she know that? She was just sure, that was all, and she had scrubbed it back to life after that day the beans boiled dry just as she had scrubbed herself back to life ... well, her back started to grip at her so much she had to get down on the board floor on her hands and knees to ease it. While she was down there, staring at the scrubbed timber, she thought how much happier she'd be if she could just make her way over to the stove where the rug was. It would be kinder to her bony knees, she thought, but it still seemed impossibly far away. But it was only a few minutes before she was able to move again and then she wondered why she had imagined the pain to be so bad. It was okay now. It was just a dull ache after all.

Hester got up from the floor and tidied some more of the table. When the next one started she tried to get to the bed. It went on like that for most of the afternoon.

No one found the baby until most a week later. Libby come across the pathetic body when she found Sally's dog pawing at the cardboard box under Solomon's cabin. First she tried shooing the dog off but it paid her no mind, worrying and worrying over the box as if it was full of prime steak. If the box hadn't been jammed in so tight the dog might have got it. As it was, Libby herself had trouble pulling it free, what with having to bend her rounded body near in two to see what was driving the dog so crazy.

'What you scratching at there boy?' she asked the dog conversationally as she got down heavily onto her knees and set to digging out the box.

It didn't smell too good and she nearly abandoned the task, assuming it might just be old throwd away bones fit for a dog. Except folks boiled up such bones into prime soup for their suppers. There wasn't much left over for a dog in these parts.

At last it come loose and Libby cleared off the cover of brown paper and rags. She and Sally's brown dog peered in together.

Sissie Jane said the little fella could not have been dead when it was born because she had seen too many of them to know otherwise. This one had breathed air, she said, you could always tell. She reckoned it was smothered with the rags it lay in.

The gossip went round like a grass fire. Young Hester killed her own baby. She birthed it all alone and then held a cloth over its face to stop it breathing. She stuffed it in a old box under the house and left it for trash. Not even a Christian burial for the poor child. Never even baptized and now destined for limbo. The tale worsened the further it traveled. Do you know she chopped the body into pieces? Who? The girl that kilt her own child. You serious? Into five pieces I heard tell. As I heard it, the dog ate the most part.

Hester, from age thirteen, became known as that girl as kilt her own child. It was after that she withdrew, spending most of her time at the spigot. Taking to sitting for hours with a book in front of her, sometimes the page not turning all day. It was never easy to tell from then on when she had her quiet fits because she often sat for hours never moving. Maybe she was off in a fit most of the time but no one liked to get too close to see. Off with God, her brother would of said if he was alive. Off with both Joe and God maybe.

I have reason to think it was the folks as turned our Hester into the gray, quiet shadow she become after that, not the killing of the baby itself. For she survived the birthing and the burying without hardly a change to her mind, but it was when the talk started she began hiding away inside of herself. Closing in, I always thought, like them big old castles that kings have in fairy tales, pulling everything inside the walls and clanking up the chain on the drawbridge so's nothing can get in. But it seem like nothing can get out neither.

And who is to say Hester wasn't in a fit when the baby come and it didn't just die waiting for someone to clear its tiny mouth of mucous?

It could be true but it ain't. Only us old ladies at the spigot kept Hester company after that, Sissie Jane, Libby and me, none of us asking for a explanation.

Joseph's mind was only half listening now as he thought about the Hester in his manuscript and realized how remote she was from the young girl Loula spoke of. And neither seemed anything to do with the slow pathetic figure that sat at the faucet in the mornings with a book open on her lap. He was frightened too, because at the back of his mind he had an idea who the eyes might belong to.

*   *   *

It was only mid afternoon when Joseph got back to his hotel and he promised himself a swim in the pool. The water was good and it allowed his thoughts to flow. But he spent the time floating rather than swimming, drifting in his thoughts, concentrating on the story once more, aware that he was tucking the eyes out of sight. He knew his manuscript was wrong, he told himself, but he was not sure how to fix it. He had put together the facts, childish stories, thinking he had known the young Hester, but Libby had drawn a different girl and he saw her now in a changed light. He needed to feel what Hester had felt, before he could move on.

He began to imagine what it must have been like for Hester, the hard times she had lived through, her family dwindling until there was just her father left, and then finding Solomon mistreating her. Joseph had trouble deciding on the word mistreat and even then he knew it was not good enough. The man had robbed the child of her life. That wasn't right. Yet they were both Joseph's own flesh and blood, Hester and Solomon. It was so difficult to take sides with one or the other. And at the back of his mind he was fighting down the thought that the eyes Hester feared might belong to his own grandfather.

Straight away Joseph shook off the idea and swam several lengths of the pool without stopping. He was exhausted by the time he allowed himself to rest and drift closer to the side of the pool. He ran his hand through his wet hair and concentrated instead on the story of Hester and Poppy that he was determined to write. He was calmer now, he told himself, and he tried again to imagine living his life as the young Hester, to feel what it must have been like for her. As his breathing eventually slowed, so the pictures began to form. Now he saw the small, skinny scrap of a child Hester, her large eyes moist and close to his own cheeks for comfort. He could hear her sniff away tears as she bent closer and whispered her words in his ear. And she was calling him Joe, he realized for the first time.

As Joseph began to see the scene in his own mind, to relive a time dredged up by the stories Old Loula had told him over the last few days, then the words of his own story started to form in his head. He wanted to write what he remembered. First he practiced sentences but soon his memory was so full he had to get out the pool and towel himself quickly, anxious to get to his room and the laptop to capture the words before they disappeared.

Back in his room he cleared away the remains of the whiskey and started afresh. He pulled on some clean jog pants and put a fresh towel round his shoulders to catch the water still dripping from his hair. He didn't feel the nightmares could catch him in the strong daylight with his body so fresh and chlorine clean.

He turned on the laptop, opened his file and this time the words spilled out, bringing with them a sadness for a young girl trapped in so many ways. His own self-pity cleared and finally he was able to write. Rather than live through his own nightmare again he found a better way to deal with the story, a way in through Hester. If it had been bad for him, he felt, it must have been worse for her. He barely thought about what he was writing and he never stopped to check through the page after page that formed on the screen in front of him. The words flowed straight to his fingers from a part of his mind that had been locked for as long as he could remember.

It was late when Joseph finally looked up and realized he was chilled. Throwing the towel into the bathroom, he pulled out a fresh sweater and put it straight on over his bare chest. He would not look at the words he had written, he decided, so he backed-up the file and went down to find out about some hot food.

*   *   *

Joseph made sure he was at the faucet early, hoping to beat Old Loula, and Hester was there waiting for him, sitting on the green striped fishing stool. He talked to her now, sure she was listening, but knowing better than to expect a reply. I've worked hard on this chapter, he said. I remember this part. You won't find it easy. But it wasn't easy for me either. Not back then. I was so small, he told her. Not that I blame you. I didn't come to understand until later, when Sally died. That was when the nightmares started and all I had was them and the memory of a girl with bruises on her face. I was just five. I don't think I could have told you back then whether I was black or white, a girl or a boy. All I seemed to have were memories of you and Poppy. Stories of Solomon and the Witchunter General.

Hester didn't look up but Joseph knew better by now than to think she might. He was just glad the book in her lap was still closed. I have something else to read you, he said, but you won't like it.

He opened the plastic file from his case and pulled out the printed pages.

Page 85.

Hester now found a better book, he read, one written in words she could make sense of, but even then it spoke more of Germany than where her own story took place. But how would that make a difference to a young child who didn't know Chicago from New York. From the vastness of America, Germany and Essex were not too far distant. Everything was a world apart from where she herself lived. Hester read the book avidly, a book telling of a Jesuit priest called Father Friedrick von Spree who traveled Germany early in the 1600's, hearing the confessions of hundreds of women as they sat in their cells, condemned to be burnt at the stake for witchcraft. As he listened to the charges brought against these women, of them flying at night on broomsticks, worshipping the devil and being bedded by Satan himself, the priest realized the stories had more to do with the diseased minds of the inquisitors than the women themselves. Father von Spree blamed the witch hunt on the two men who had written the Hammer of the Witches and also on Pope Innocent VIII who had allowed the church to become involved. Von

Spree watched as the whole of his country burned with the fire and smoke of executions. He wrote that 10,000 females were put to death and many were under the age of ten.

Hester's stomach felt heavy as a stone when she read this. Suddenly it seemed very real to her. She imagined herself in a dark cell, giving her last confession for witchcraft to Father von Spree.

The floor was covered with straw and very little light came in from the barred window high above. She was trying to explain to Father von Spree that she had not done it, that she couldn't fly a broomstick, that the devil had never been to her bed, that he would never fit his great wings and tail into her small trundle bed although she felt she knew the word bedding had more to do with Solomon's fumblings between her legs than her bed itself. She was trying to say she didn't speak German, that he would not be able to understand her confession and she would never be saved as Sissie Jane promised they would all be saved, so she tried instead to sing one of Sissie's loud gospel praises. But when the Father spoke to her it wasn't in German. She found she understood his words in the darkness of that small cell but she was barely listening because the stench suddenly overpowered her senses and all she could think of was keeping out the smell before her stomach heaved. Then she noticed the straw on the floor and saw it was not fresh and golden as she had thought, but rotted and black where the urine had wetted it through and still it wasn't enough to hold back the puddles and streams that ran across the floor. With horror she realized the foul mixture of vomit, sweat and excrement was her own.

She tried to move but the chains held her back. As her other senses gradually returned she found her hands hurt where the heavy iron cuffs dug into her flesh. She looked down at the weeping sores on her wrists and ankles and knew she had been here longer than she realized. If she had not spurned Nathaniel then perhaps none of this would have happened.

'Don't speak so,' said the woman beside her in a gentle voice. For a moment Poppy thought it was Heliotrope but then she remembered it was Sarah Fletcher, her lovely Sarah, now sitting matted and huddled, chained to the wall. 'Don't speak so,' she repeated and then fell into a coughing fit. The damp cell was an unhealthy place, full only of bad air and bad omen, thought Poppy.

When the blow caught Poppy across the face it took her by surprise. Her mind had been wandering and she had forgotten where she was. It wasn't Father von Spree in front of her but her inquisitor, the Witchunter General who sat unmoving on a stool. The guard stood over Poppy with his hand raised and ready.

'Confess you are in league with the Devil himself and you can be saved,' demanded her inquisitor quietly, as Poppy groped to pull herself upright. The pain in her jaw layered down through old bruises and she fought back tears as she waited for it to dull. The cut over her eye had opened once more and blood was trickling fast down her cheek. She could taste its salt.

'It will do you no good to be stubborn because you stand accused, witch. Or maybe you are a Jew, is that it? We have two Jew girls here already and they say you and your friend Sarah here are pork haters.'

'But Sarah eats no meat at all,' started Poppy, knowing she was repeating words that no one listened to, words that had not freed them over the last weeks. Nathaniel had her arrested for witchcraft but it was now all wrapped up with Sarah's being condemned for a Jew. None of it made sense any more.

'For you must know how it be against the law to worship as a Jew,' said the Witchunter again. 'I only want to save your soul,' he repeated patiently. 'You will thank me eventually.'

'But I be not a Jew,' pleaded Poppy, the phrase now almost without meaning because she had repeated it so many times. Her head span with words and blurred pictures and she fought to match them into pairs. The solid matches were easier; sheep, cows, dogs, it was the gossamer couples that eluded her. Analyzing one word, she thought, a simple word like foot, saying it over and over in your mind made you wonder what it was supposed to represent. Did it mean anything at all, she wondered, or was it just a sound. How was it that whole communities and races of people came to agree that a certain noise meant anything at all? The name foot, multiplied until it dazzled you, seemed suddenly too full of air to ever take the weight of a whole person. It was all nonsense she decided. Like the word Jew. She no longer knew nor cared what it stood for. It was so close to the gentle word of dew, that magic water mist that used to greet her every morning as she threw back the sack door of their house in the marshes, a part of her life she was finding harder to recall, that surely it could not harm her. If she just agreed, said yes, told them she was a dew, she had always been dew, and bathed on a Saturday night but could not abide the taste of pork, then surely they would let her home to see Heliotrope again.

Another blow sent her sprawling across the floor as far as her chains would allow and she heard Sarah gasp and then choke again.

'Tell the truth,' whispered the Witchunter, 'for yourself and the old woman. You both stand accused and it be my concern to get the truth confessed. Will you sign now or will I leave you to the guards again? Jews and witches be heretics alike and heretics we can have no time for. Confess for yourself and give me the names of the others. I will bring you all to God, that is what I dam here to do.'

How much worse could it be if she confessed, she thought, although she knew the answer. To be condemned meant a hanging, but so did confession. Their only hope was to be thought innocent and released. Over the past weeks Poppy had chanted everything she remembered of the Bible as proof of her Christianity but it seems she garbled as much Old Testament as anything else, adding to the accusation of her being a Jew, making it worse, and she was now so tired she was in danger of confusing the old gods into her rambled, blurred speech. The more frightened she became, the more difficult it was to work out what the answers should be. Two girls from the village, themselves under torture, had accused Sarah of being a Jew because she refused to eat meat, but now it seemed Poppy was under suspicion too, all because she was in the habit of cleaning herself, and like Sarah she changed her underclothes once a week. If only they had foreseen a danger they could easily have made Friday or Sunday the day they changed their linen for fresh. They had been so careful in other things but had never seen the danger of the Jewish Sabbath. It was true that Poppy could not take pork, it always made her sick.

Poppy was lost in her own thoughts and it came as a surprise to find the Withchunter General had gone and two guards were grabbing her, one under the arms, the other holding tight to her feet while she was unshackled from the wall. They carried, half dragged her from the cell and the last thing she remembered was the soft sad whimpering sound coming from where Sarah Fletcher sat huddled. They both knew things were about to get worse.

Poppy wasn't thinking clearly, it was all a haze, unreal. She stumbled along a narrow passageway between the guards and when they came to some circular stone steps the chain linking her leg shackles was too short to let her walk down. But the guards never slackened their pace so she was dragged and pulled until they reached the corridor at the bottom, but she never regained her footing before they came to a closed room. There were no windows, no light except the two torches which hung from one wall. Just light enough to see the awfulness of the place but you could have guessed without seeing, thought Poppy, because the smell of fear oozed with the water that trickled from the walls.

'The truth flows faster from a young maid's lips in this room that any other,' said the older of the two guards with a chuckle as he fastened her hand irons to a metal ring on the wall. Then he spat in the corner. He was fat, unshaven and as unwashed as Poppy feared she now was herself. His hands were large and heavy, black hairs growing on the back of them and right up his fingers. He began to unknot the top of her bodice. The other guard was a lot younger and stood a little way off as if he was afraid to join in. He was uncommonly tall but as thin as a broomstick handle, she thought, trying to focus her mind on anything other than the filthy hands of the older guard.

Poppy had been afraid of Nathaniel's probing hands but she was fast learning that there were worse things.

'You got to tell the truth, see,' said the younger guard, although he didn't seem convinced that this was a good enough argument, 'else Pug,' and he nodded towards the other guard, 'else Pug here gets carried away.' He was tapping the tips of his fingers together, quickly, first tip against tip and then finger pad against the nails of the other hand. He couldn't keep his long thin body still. He began to sway from side to side, his weight changing from foot to foot.

The rough hands of Pug had already removed her bodice and were pulling her shift clear of her shoulders. With her hands chained he could not remove it.

The younger one was close shaven, and when the other called him over she heard his name was Fred. Poppy was determined to look at something and Fred was the better of the two. He was neat, pink faced and he blushed as he saw her exposed. She looked briefly at Pug, but not his hands. He was gray bristled and his crumpled clothes looked as if he slept in them, which he probably did, and his fingernails were clogged with grime.

Pug tried to undo the ties to her skirt but very soon he grew tired of the knots and cut the strings. She felt it drop to the ground. He then called Fred over and told him to take off her clothing. He came towards her and started pulling at the strings of her petticoats but his fingers were clumsy and Pug laughed at him. Finally the young, red-faced Fred took a long knife from the table and cut those strings too, so the layers of cotton fell loose and he could pull them down over the chains on her feet. It was the first time Poppy had looked at the table. It was littered with metal tools as big as those the blacksmith in Mistley used for shoeing horses. And there were candles there too, and flints, but she doubted they were intended to give light, and the fear of burning skin made her sick in the pit of her stomach.

Poppy was standing in just a shift. It was unbelievably cold on the stone floor and she was too frightened to bother concealing her smaller leg or arm from view. They knew of the birthmark already and there was nothing else to hide from them. They were both laughing at the withered leg and they began to play with her. Pug snatched the knife and used the tip of the blade to raise up her chin so she could no longer hide her chest away in the hunch of her shoulders. It meant she must look up away from him and she decided this was best as well. She tried to picture her home, groping for the friendly warmth of mud walls to replace the hostile stone that surrounded her now, but the more she tried to remember the trees the less she could find the meaning of green in her head and it sent her into a panic. Instead of the wooded homely scene she sought, Sarah's grimed face and knotted hair came to her and was enough to knock from her own head any belief that there had ever been another life, that she had really lived with a small bubbly woman called Sarah in their clearing near Mistley Thorn and Tendring Hundred.

Then Poppy was pushed roughly onto a small stool and another pair of hands, someone she had not known was in the room, forced a metal implement over her head and she felt a heavy iron lever being pressed into her mouth. It gripped her tongue and forced it down, clamping against her jaw and making her gag. She couldn't move her head at all and the iron was being screwed tighter and tighter until she couldn't tell which hurt more, the pain in her jaw or the fear in her bowels. She tried desperately to focus on something else, something more real, or less real, she couldn't make up her mind. The young guard was frightened now, she could see his face and his small pale hands.

She tried to picture Tabby sitting on her lap. How Tabby had loved to be petted, her silky hair sleek and smooth and Poppy following the tortoiseshell designs over her back. Somewhere in her head she knew that pattern was waiting for her. If only she could picture it now and trace her finger across that small cat back and up between those neat ears then she could block out what the guard was doing. She tried but it wouldn't come. Poppy nearly cried to think the very picture of Tabby was slipping away from her. What did she look like? What shape was a cat? Any cat? Perhaps she didn't know. The harder she tried the worse it became. The word cat took on no meaning when she slid it past her mind and no picture formed at all. Tabby and cat had been wiped clean from her head as surely as a stream might wash clean the mud from her hands. Poppy tried to hold an image of running water but even this was slipping away.

The other guard, Pug, was dribbling, and hands she couldn't see were working away from behind her, forcing something into her mouth, strips of linen, she thought, and when she refused to swallow he pulled her backwards into his arms and held a pitcher of water to her mouth, drowning her and making the material gag in her throat. Even through it all she smelt the smell of him, his sweat, his power, as pitcher after pitcher of water was tipped into her mouth and she gasped for air, desperate to swallow anything that was keeping her from breathing. She no longer thought of anything except the fight for her next breath.

Poppy grasped on to anything that would help her live through to the next second, the next minute and she dreaded to think if she could survive much longer than that. She knew that hell did not exist. When her time came at last, and she was ceasing to care that this might happen soon, then she would meet all of her gods and there would be nothing to fear in that, for she had respected them well over her few years. She had sacrificed food to them and rejoiced in the ritual dances of the feast days.

She wanted desperately to leave her body, a thing she had found so easy as a child but which eluded her now whenever she craved it most. She tried to remember Heliotrope's face but her life before this place was slipping away from her and she was powerless to stop it. Maybe she had never lived outside this prison. Perhaps Heliotrope did not exist. This would be her life now, split between the tedium of waiting in the gloomy stone room and living moment by moment through the horror of what they might do to her body.

An hour must have gone by and Poppy never imagined anyone could live this long. The ends of the strips of linen hung from her mouth until there was no room to force in another and yet still it went on. The water was so heavy in her stomach she could feel her insides swollen and bursting with it and she was choking constantly to cough out what had slipped into her lungs. And knowing they would pull out the strips when they were done was enough to make her wish she might die instead.

* * *

Joseph stopped reading. For a moment he thought Hester was in a petit

153

mal fit, she seemed so still; then he looked more closely and saw the tears collecting on the end of her nose and dripping into her lap. Unsure of how to help he put the pages on the seat beside him and went over to pick up one of her hands. They stayed like that, untalking, Joseph hunkered down beside the short fishing stool, until Old Loula came into the clearing after a while.

Thankful of the interruption Joseph stood up and tidied away his papers. He patted Hester on the shoulder before walking over and drawing the water for Old Loula. For the first time he began to see what he might be doing to Hester herself. Did he really have the right to put her through more, just to free himself? He didn't know, he decided, so he excused himself and went for a walk, trying to puzzle out how a young girl could cope with the life Hester had been dealt and expect to live through it sane. He wanted to know more about Hester's dead baby, too. It was something he had avoided asking Old Loula up till now but he might broach it if she was still there when he got back.

Chapter 16

Joseph drove into town and phoned his office to arrange more holiday with his secretary. There were a few appointments but they seemed so unimportant down here, so far from the city hustle, and he dealt quickly with the problems and rang off. Then he went back to the small store and selected a fishing rod and some hooks, taking advice from the store owner about the bait he would need for the creek. He deserved to go fishing at some point, he decided, it was a holiday after all.

It was getting late and Joseph wanted to get back to a supper at the hotel, thinking the fishing trip could wait a day, but something at the back of his mind told him he was just avoiding the visit to Sally's cabin down by the creek. So instead he drove back to the clearing once more, parked the car and took the fishing gear out of the trunk. He wasn't even sure he knew the way to the cabin. It had been a long time and he had been so young.

It was turning evening now and Joseph was surprised to find Old Loula still out on the seat. Did she never do anything else? He walked over and she seemed to be expecting him.

I didn't tell you all I could of about the baby, she said, even before he had time to say good evening. He hadn't meant to stop but he felt obliged now to sit down.

In her own mind she didn't do it, Old Loula told him, and he presumed she was talking about Hester.

How could she of smothered it when it was dead anyway, Old Loula asked him. That was the way she was thinking, see, she said. She had kilt the baby that day in the crick with the lye soap and the scrubbing brush and the gin after. And that wasn't killing because the girls from the town called it aborting and with a word like that it must be different. And even if she did hold the cloth over its mouth it was only to keep it from crying out on account of she didn't want to hear the sound of the thing she had kilt with the lye.

I have puzzled it all, Old Loula told him.

And because it was never born, just aborted, it didn't count. But the way Hester saw it, it was dead all that time from the day with the lye until the spring. She just knew.

She looked in its eyes and he was there, just as she knew he would be. The eyes was shining out at her, taunting. The small arms would of waved, clenching and unclenching them tiny fingers into fists. She had to get that cloth over its mouth quick to keep in the noise of the lye and the gin. It had been dead all them months, she would of known that, but it was important to keep it quiet. She had kept it quiet all them months already. A little more would do no harm.

So she kept the noise in and at last the long dead fetus, because that was what it was called and she would of learned that word from hearing Sissie Jane talking to women from the town, at last the fetus kept its arms still. That was better. She could get it into the box at last. However could she of got it in the box if it hadn't been still? That was okay. That would make everything better.

Old Loula was quiet for a while. A small breeze rippled up but it didn't clear the tension in the air. Joseph took a deep breath and plunged into his own nightmare. He had to ask. It was the one thing he needed to know.

Whose eyes were they? He asked.

I don't know, said Old Loula eventually. I've never known.

The two of them sat for some time without talking until Old Loula finally stood up and walked off.

Joseph didn't know if he had the strength to look inside himself any more. The eyes frightened him more than he was willing to acknowledge but he didn't really know why. It was just tied up with him sitting on the rug in the cabin and a scrap of a girl who told him stories and cuddled him to her when she cried. And what he was most afraid of, he finally admitted to himself, was that if the eyes belonged to Solomon, his own grandfather, then where did that put him? If a girl would abort a baby to keep those eyes from hurting society again, they must be beyond evil. And did he have a part of those eyes in his own genes? Was it just men who were a threat? Was that why he had not started a family of his own? Was that the fear he carried inside him, that he too might turn into something … what was the word in his head, the analogy some child had told him so many years before?

He puzzled it for a while, drawing the thing out by a thread, half willing it to come to mind and half wanting to push it back where it could no longer hurt him.

Joseph wasn't really in the mood for fishing now but he found himself standing up and collecting the fishing gear around him. He watched himself walking purposefully into the trees, heading for where he believed the creek and the cabin were waiting for him.

Hitler, his brain said suddenly. It was another Hitler Hester had been so frightened of. He could hear the words in his head, her childish voice explaining over and over to him why she had done it. It wasn't a baby, she had told him, it was a monster, another Hitler. Joseph thought he must have known it all along.

He stopped for a moment and leant against a tree for support. What if Hester had been right, he thought, or even believed she was right? What an awesome responsibility for a child. But who else could have helped her? What would any sane person have done if she had told them her fears, that she was letting loose a monster, that the eyes inside her were so awful she couldn't let them live? Joseph had never understood before why Hester had offloaded her own problems on to him, and he'd resented every nightmare he had lived through on her behalf. Now he was readjusting his thoughts to see it from the other side. If Hester was forced to take the decision alone to keep away the eyes, to send them back to a pool of unborn spirits and make them wait another chance to come into the world, then how much damage would that do to her own mind? And no one could ever say for sure that she wasn't right about the baby she carried, because it never lived to threaten the world. Hester may just have sacrificed her own life to save another holocaust, and this was all the thanks she got.

Who could ever make that level of decision about an unborn and unknown child, he wondered, and who in the world would ever thank them for making it? What persecution could the mother of Hitler have expected if she had killed her child before his hatred had developed and damaged the whole world, killing those millions of people and almost destroyed an entire race? Would it have been just another headline in the local newspaper? Young mother kills own baby. Child murder shock. Infanticide. He wondered how many times that may have happened throughout time.

Joseph felt a chill for the second time that warm, balmy evening and knew the world would see it differently after the event, when the damage had already been unleashed. To rid the world of a Jack the Ripper, a Pol Pot, a Saddam Hussein, or a Stalin before they were even born would deserve the Nobel Peace Prize at least, he thought. Hindsight might be a wonderful thing but society was very skeptical of foresight.

Joseph didn't know quite what to make of this new piece of information that his memory had spat out for him. It didn't explain whose eyes Hester associated with her unborn child, only that she had felt them to be so inexplicably destructive. But if she had really felt the child would grow to be such a threat, then what choices did she really have? Or was she just a mad girl who killed a child because she knew no better?

Joseph played with words in his head, guessing up one avenue of thought and down another, not noticing as he pushed himself away from the tree and let his feet carry him steadily towards the creek.

* * *

Joseph was a little surprised to find the cabin so easily. It was nearer the creek than he remembered, and the tall trees the young boys used to climb and shout down names at him were oddly small, insignificant, their out of reach branches now low and easily scaled.

He looked at the cabin for a moment but was reluctant to go any closer. It was sadly derelict. Sally would have been upset he knew. With the thoughts of Hester and the eyes still catapulting round his head, Joseph turned instead towards the creek and looked for a spot to set up his fishing, determined to be excited by his new rod and to get Hester and Poppy out of his head for a while.

He fished for an hour or so but then he found the words drifting in his mind were of Poppy again, but this time he remembered other stories told to him by Hester, of Poppy and Tom and love, and he wanted to work on these happier parts of his book. Using the new fishing knife he cut a small tree branch and fashioned the v shape to make a rest for his rod, so he could write and fish at the same time. He placed this firmly in the ground and wedged the rod against it. But it wasn't right yet, he needed more control, to be in contact in case something took the bait.

It took a while to get the system going but eventually he took off his shoes and found a way of sitting hard against a tree trunk and placing the rod between his toes with the other foot behind for support, and the main weight taken by the v stick. Then he picked up his pen and notepad and began to work on the better times for Poppy. He owed it to Hester.

It was the most pleasant few hours of Joseph's stay. He was so engrossed he was startled to find Old Loula walking towards him. It was odd to see her anywhere other than at the seat by the faucet, he thought, and then realized it was a stupid thing to think. He hadn't noticed how dark it was getting either, or how much he was straining to see the words as he wrote.

He watched as Old Loula came up to him and hunkered down near the riverbank, wondering if she had come out on purpose to speak to him. This was obviously the case because she gave no preamble, no small talk, but lurched into her storytelling as if they had been sitting together for some time.

When I tell you this next part, she said, you will realize it hit me hard. You may have guessed by now how Solomon meant a lot to me, for all he married some other woman. She straightened her worn skirt and then shuffled uncomfortably on the ground so it wrinkled again anyway. Joseph concentrated on what she was saying. He had to know more about Solomon, to find out what he was like, to see if the eyes were connected to his own family.

It hit me hard, him marrying some other woman, Old Loula repeated. Sometimes life just works out like that. I lost Solomon more than once, you see, so the second time it was doubly hard to bear.

It was unusual for Solomon to be at the spigot of an evening, she told him. He wanted to be with his wife is the way I see it now, to ask her forgiveness, and sitting on the bench he had made for us women seemed as near a place as any he could think of. I imagine he watched the steady drip of water much as I do now. It has a kind of therapy for me, that drip.

It was late and dark, not long after that time with Hester and the dead baby being found. Most folks was inside for the night but, like as not, some young boys might of walked out into the clearing from the creek road. I imagine they was laughing and you might think they'd been sitting up a tree at Sally's place, except Sally did no entertaining them days. One of them boys prob'ly picked up a stick and threw it as far as he could.

Solomon would of watched the arc of the stick and listened to the boys talking. That was two sons he hisself had lost now, two sons, a wife and most part of his daughter, for what was left of Hester was small and hollow, like there was nobody home.

Maybe Solomon tried to remember hisself as a young man again and if so then I reckon the pictures in his head would be like a movie film of someone else. It would be hard for him to recall how he had once loved a young girl called Loula in those day before that old pail, the enamel one with the blue piped rim. The whole thing between Solomon, Young Loula and the enamel pail was one big misunderstanding. But once it had gone wrong it seems there was no fixing it back together. A humpty dumpty of a tale.

I may be the best one to be piecing Hester's story together on account of I wasted my life too. I had it good to start but then I threw it away for pride.

Old and chipped that pail is now, but it was not always that way. I recall a day when it was new and shiny and just about as valuable a courting present as a sensible young man could of thought to bring a coy young lady as wanted to furnish up the cabin she was now making her own. My Ma and Aunt Violet had both passed on and the place was mine to call my own. It was also the only cabin around with a single, lone, eligible young woman in it, living by herself, which some considered a mite scandalous on account of in those days we was not as broad minded as today.

It was so very nice to start adding small touches to the cabin that was my own furnishings, not the possessions of my Ma. Long before I got that enamel pail I was organizing the house the way I wanted. The period of mourning and respect for Ma was short on account of there not being much to grieve over. I had done all that for my Aunt Violet just the year before and, besides, I was fond of Aunt Violet. Certainly more attached to Violet than I ever was to my Ma who, it must be said, I was plain pleased to see the back of in the end. There was a time we might talk civil to each other, mother to daughter like, but that had been some time back. Before my figure begun to develop bulges and curves to outshine the glory of my elders and betters to put none too fine a point on it. Because my elders and betters, as they cared to call theyselves, had always considered they was cute young things too, until the young men's eyes started wandering away from their own close fitted print dresses and lingering on mine. And it was only seeing just how high my nipples jutted through my cotton shifts that made them realize how theirs had lowered. My Ma and Aunt Violet started to look at each other's butts then, and the two sisters would look at each other and then look at my own round, high, taut buns as I was learning how to sass for the boys. After that my Ma was mean to her daughter Loula, and Violet soon learned it was near impossible to remain neutral and only common sense to side with the party as provided the roof over her head. Added to that, she also found she needed someone to blame for the waning attention she was getting from the men folk that had once found her a beauty. All in all Aunt Violet and me was only friends here and there, in small moments, private times when my Ma was otherwise occupied.

So when they had both passed on and I was left to live all alone in the cabin I became quite a focus, and many of the boys would whittle me pegs or chop wood for me in the hope of winning a favor. I just loved all that attention, course I did for I was never a shy girl, but there was only one boy I really wanted and he never came by the cabin at all. The more Solomon ignored me, the more passionate I became about wanting him.

The pail itself was my downfall is the way I see it. That pail and greed. Whispers I heard over the years told how I carted it round as a love trophy but, like many whispers, it couldn't be further from the truth. The pail was a self-imposed penance that I give myself so I would never again be greedy for worldly goods. The purpose was to remind me the better importance of people and love over possessions. It didn't work of course and I sometimes curse that old pail for shouting my shattered dream at me every day of my life and when I overhear folks say I is a sharp, bitter old woman I fear it may be as that old pail has made sure I never have been able to forget how I spoiled my own chance of happiness. I never could decide if I loved that old pail or hated the very sight of it.

Solomon was a handsome man when he was young, though he was fearsome shy. One day I saw him across the creek and shouted out.

'Solomon,' I said, 'you may just feel inclined to stop by and taste some pie I made.'

I said it casual like, sounding as if I didn't care if he called back yes or no but my chest fluttered inside me and I had to keep myself from looking directly at him in case he saw. Instead, I held a dry flower stem to my mouth and blew the seeds off into the wind. The prettiness of the picture could not have been lost on Solomon, I swear. But I know now, to my cost, that he couldn't believe I meant it truly, thinking maybe I was teasing him on account of him being poor and me having some other beau callers as could swank and talk right and even wear shoes, not the great boots folk in these parts wore if they bothered to cover their feet with anything at all. For this reason, it seems, he decided I was laughing at him and he did not believe that I meant for him to take seriously the visit that was offered.

I just wish I had knowed that back then. I waited in all that afternoon and the evening too, listening out for Solomon. Maybe he didn't have the grace and sweet talk of the others but Solomon, back then, had the sure build I saw again in his son Joe. So I waited in, anxious but dressed pretty as a picture, and Solomon never did come. That was the start of the pout on my pretty lips, even I concede that. And as the years passed it would grind great furrows in the sides of my cheeks and cut ridges from where my eyebrows near met, up into my hairline. I have watched them grow in the glass I keep by the bed. That was the first time I ever was jilted and I didn't like it.

From then on I tried to tell myself Solomon was a great clumsy oaf of a man anyroad and I would have no more to do with him even if he begged me. I am ashamed to admit I daydreamed about him begging me, just to make sure I would be strong enough to rebuff him, as I reckoned the practice would be good for me. So I imagined him, pained with love for me, at the door of my cabin, begging for just a seat at the table and the chance to talk awhile.

'No,' I would practice. 'You had the chance Solomon and you humiliated me in refusing it.' That is what I would tell him when he finally came to apologize to me.

Over and over in my mind I practiced turning on my heel, flying into the cabin and slamming the door. Sometimes there may be variations, like I might see myself turning back to him first, trying a sad smile and then closing the cabin door firmly in his face so he could suffer the same as I had. Then I would go to my bedroom. That was where it always ended though, never going further. In the daydream nothing was resolved.

It pains me to confess this now but I lived that daydream all summer long, taking on a hurt that was never intended it seems, and it was getting into the wet weather again before I really allowed my many beaux to come woo me once more. There was one in particular, a traveling man with a dandy cotton blazer that looked for all the world like he had stepped right from the streets of Harlem and found hisself in this two cent backwoods by mistake. It was him, Bo Rogers he called hisself, as brought the pail.

I see now that Bo Rogers knew the value of such a prized item to a girl with no shoes on her feet, for he never come with the pail on the first visit. Like as not he knew I may not part with the purchase price straight off, for he was traveling sales folk and bartering come natural to him. Bo Rogers did not intend to be short-changed on the deal. I recall I met Bo several times before I asked him back for a piece of my pie. He played the gentleman that first time at my cabin, and the next, although he allowed the idea of a present to settle itself as he took his leave the second time.

It was on the third visit he brought the shiny, perfect pail along with him.

'I was just on my way delivering, Miss Loula, and I stopped by with the pleasurable intent of seeing you once again,' he said. 'You are free?' he inquired.

'Yes. Please do come in,' I said, but I was flustered from having no pie or bake, nor even some bacon or coffee to give him.

He made certain I seen the pail straight off as he dangled it by the smooth wood grip through which the metal handle passed. That pail swung to and fro like a pendulum ticking away the time.

'That is a mighty fine pail,' I told him.

'It most certainly is of the highest quality,' he said and the words were practiced like he told them a hundred times, and like as not he had got hisself a easy piece of young skirt on account of them words and that line of pail. 'You see that enamel?' he asked me, holding it up so as I could see. 'Thick as my finger. Won't chip none if you keep that pail the rest of your life Miss Loula.'

I was hesitating, and with good reason because it turned out that was a lie.

'This pail is guaranteed,' he added. It was his clinch line and I was young and vulnerable.

I could see the glint in his eye and the way his smile took on a lop-sided leer but, to be honest, I was that embarrassed at having no coffee in the place I was almost glad to distract him with a small show of my charms. As it turned out, the pail come more expensive than I expected.

At least he had the grace to leave me the pail when he sneaked out the cabin later that night. That's how I come to see it in the end. He could of took the pail as well and left me nothing to be bitter about. This way I had something to blame the rest of my life. No one need ever of known of course, except the way Nature has of being spiteful. Some folks can wait years for a child. Certainly Solomon and his wife were to think they might never be blessed until Joe finally came by after all them years of barren nights but it was my bad luck, like so many girls, to fall the first time. Mother Nature likes a laugh I have noticed.

I kept the abortion quiet and few folk knew much was amiss, except Solomon hisself. It was his mother was the only one I could turn to in them days. Sissie Jane was just a slip of a girl herself and not yet into doctoring the way she does now. Solomon's mother was the only one I could think of as would know what to do, and it turned out she did. The price I had to pay was Solomon, of course. Even then it was misunderstanding all over again.

I believed I had shamed myself beyond Solomon wanting me by then, yet it turned out he would have stood by me. Even at my lowest, shamed, carrying another man's child out of wedlock and reduced to lying in his mother's cabin while she took her knitting needles to me, he considered his beautiful Loula was out of his reach. Pity was, neither of us said a word. We went our separate ways after that, Solomon marrying a homely girl and me starting my lonely life with that damn pail for company.

Well, this isn't getting Hester's story told, she said after a long pause.

I was saying how Solomon sat out on the bench that night and must of watched young boys throwing their stick like they did most evenings them days. I think he must of sat there long after that but no one saw him. I have run this through my head on sleepless nights until I feel I know every step Solomon took that night.

Solomon got up and walked in the direction of his gin shack thinking he might take a drink first, to steady him, but then he decided it would be best to meet his maker sober. He no longer dreamed of meeting his wife.

Solomon carried on walking toward the shack because that was where he kept the rope. He never was a bad man; it was just that life went wrong for him so many times. He didn't know how to do it better. He never could feel sure about hisself after the way he fell in love with a young girl named Loula, the way she made him long for her and then laughed at him for doing so. And his wife knew all them years that her husband went on loving another woman. Solomon would of given anything to have loved his wife, for she was a good woman, but the power of Young Loula's scorn hung over their marriage. His wife tried so long to give him a family and it destroyed Solomon when she died, because he only knew then that he loved her all along. And it was too late for her to see him discover it. It was Solomon as put the bench at the spigot for her, hoping she could see from where she looked down, and it always pleased him that Hester chose that place to spend her time.

'Water,' his wife had said the night she died. Well there isn't a great deal of water round these parts, unless you count the crick, so Solomon made a bench and set it up beside the water spigot.

He wanted to stop all that business with the strap and Hester's legs but it wasn't something he could find a end to. Now he wished he'd thought of it sooner. If only he had done this at the start then maybe it would all have been all right.

Solomon's last regret before he kicked away the stool was of never seeing his wife again, I know this for sure. He would of been certain she was waiting for him in the wrong place, see?

When Clem first found Solomon strung up in the lean-to gin store he thought for a moment he was lynched. But who would lynch a man for fathering his own grandchild when such things happen all the time round here? Folks would say you can't criticize a man for making use of his own daughter. There was only one man as blamed Solomon and that was hisself. It turned out Solomon was more upset by it than most anyone else. It happened too frequent to concern the local folk, who could forgive such a thing easy enough but who wondered at the monster of a young girl as would smother her own baby. Hester was seldom regarded charitably after that.

Well, said Old Loula after a long pause, I would consider it a favor if the first part of that story were not repeated to a soul seeing as how I spent these long years keeping it quiet.

Joseph nodded but it was dark now, with just the light shining down from the moon, and he wasn't sure she saw his acknowledgment. Joseph hadn't understood the relevance of the tale to start; it was only as she drew to a close he realized Old Loula was showing him the good side of Solomon.

That's a thing off my mind anyroad, said Old Loula, and she tried to get her old legs to straighten her up but Joseph had to help her stand. She bent down and massaged the life back into her limbs. Can you find your way back in the dark, he asked? I have a flashlight here somewhere he said, and he rummaged in his new fishing bag for it.

Are you not coming, she wanted to know? But he told her he would stay a while and she said in that case he would need the light because the electric was not connected at Sally's place. If she couldn't get back home in the dark after all these years of practice then she deserved all she got, she told him, so not to worry.

As Old Loula walked away she called back to him, apologizing for the derelict state of Sally's cabin. No one would use it for all its grandness, she told him, because it was tainted by Sally.

Not that she wasn't a good woman, she added. It's just we didn't see it then, for the prejudice. But these things change, she said.

He waited until the last sound of Old Loula's footsteps had died away and then he packed away his fishing gear. The moon was shining brighter now the darkness was complete, so he decided against getting out the flashlight and stumbled his way to the cabin. The porch was as he knew it would be, the shape, the feel of it, although it was rotting away from lack of care and everything was smaller than he remembered. It was the smell that was different though, not the rose of Sally's perfume or the lavender of her floor polish, but the damp mould of decay. Sally would have died of shame.

Joseph pulled at the door into the main house, expecting it to be locked, but it creaked on old tired hinges and swung open. He imagined the young kids would play here, brave during the light of day.

It was dark inside, even though the moon shone through panes of mostly broken glass, and the ghosts of his nightmares threatened him again. He found the flashlight and switched it on. He didn't really know what he had come here to do so he walked in to the kitchen, fished out his notebook and looked round for somewhere to sit. He might as well record the way he was feeling, he thought.

It was then he noticed the green rug on the kitchen floor, the circular one with the green tassels around it, the rug he saw in his mind each time the nightmare came back. A part of him still wanted to run, to escape, but the other side talked to himself calmly and walked his grown-up body over to the mildewed rug on the floor and made it sit down beside those childish chubby legs. Man and boy sat there together, their fears the same, and waited for the eyes to taunt them again.

Joseph expected something to happen but nothing did. His heart was beating fast but the fear did not engulf him. In fact, after a short while it eased and he breathed a little deeper, the damp smell from the rug and walls easing away. But no ghosts appeared, not Sally's or any others. Maybe he would survive it, he tried to reassure himself, because part of him had intended all along to spend the night here, to face up to the nightmares once and for all.

Time slipped by and he became uncomfortable, but he was still loathe to leave the rug that played such a large part in his memory. He solved the problem by pulling the rug over to the wall so he could lean his back against it and relax a little. He was reading through his notebook, checking what he had written earlier in the evening while he was fishing. He focused again on the better times for Poppy and he wanted to write more about her and Tom because he knew the good times were so precious. He scribbled a few notes, planning his chapter for tomorrow.

Gradually he sunk back into the story but most of the ideas played in his head rather than on the paper.

Joseph didn't know how much time had gone by but it must have been several hours. He was almost at the end of his notebook now and the flashlight didn't seem as bright. Typical, he thought, the new battery running low already. Damn, it must have been old stock in the store. He should have known. He could have bought spares. Joseph scribbled down the words as the flashlight started to flicker.

Suddenly he stopped writing. He'd heard a noise, maybe a voice, maybe not, from somewhere inside the cabin. He tried to rationalize, recalling the sound in his head, worrying about it now it had stopped. He practiced the echo of the sound again, running it through his memory to check it out. Yes it could have been a voice, he decided, a very young girl, something high pitched, more like a child really.

Joseph put down his notepad and pen and moved the flashlight from where it was resting uncomfortably on his shoulder. He gently massaged the ache from his neck while he thought what to do, then he shook some life back into the flashlight and stood up. How bad could it be, he figured, just some local kids most likely, but he still found it difficult to take more than two steps across the wooden floor before his feet froze and his heart began to thump. He stayed like that for a few moments, his ears straining for a repeat of the sound and his feet ready to fly out of the cabin if it came again. Not that he thought outside would be much safer.

Joseph listened carefully but it was quiet now. He willed his feet to start again and dragged them heavily across the kitchen floor and through to the dark corridor leading down to Sally's bedroom. He felt he should be braver, he was over six foot tall he told himself, but the thought didn't ease the tightness of his breathing or the pain from his chest. The floorboards were rotten here, the smell of decayed wood hit him again as he shuffled along the passage and waited for his weight to send him through the floor.

He shook the flashlight again and saw Sally's door was ajar. He thought he saw something else too, a shadow maybe, or the shape of a man standing taller than himself, cloaked and gaunt, a dark mask hooded over most of his head like an executioner. Joseph felt his own sweat pouring into his clothes and soaking him through with a mixture of hot and clammy cold, but he still couldn't move. He wanted to close his eyes, to blink even, willing the shadow to disappear or turn back into a plain plank door, but instead the form became clearer and the eyes stared out from the two holes in the dark hood. It was then a voice whispered in his ear, maybe from inside his head or maybe from outside, and Joseph didn't know which frightened him more.

The voice was a young girl's, bending near him and breathing her soft tearful stories into his head, telling him of the hooded man, wetting his neck with warm tears. And suddenly he knew why the eyes were so important. In a black hood, the eyes shone out with great clarity. Poppy and Hester both had those eyes etched firmly in their heads. It was Poppy's Witchunter General that terrified Hester and had filtered down to his own nightmares. He had always screamed himself awake before the eyes came into focus but now he could see them clearly, shining out at him from the stories lodged in his mind.

A shriek made him jump, nearly out of his skin, then something shot past Joseph's feet and ran behind him, making a beeline for the kitchen. For a moment he thought his heart would stop but then he calmed down enough to realize it was just a cat. He looked back to where the bedroom door was swaying gently and saw only the dark wood of a high cupboard where the eyes had been looking out at him from the shadows. It was only a cat, he told himself over and over, just a cat cornered and more frightened than him most likely. No, he corrected, he was definitely the more terrified of the two of them. Yet, at the same time, he had come close to his own greatest fear and maybe now it could fade a little.

The eyes of his and Hester's nightmares belonged to the Witchunter General, he told himself again. So now he knew. It wasn't Solomon that frightened Hester, it was the real fear of an evil soul. And what if she was right? He blocked that thought out quickly. It was going to be a long night as it was, frightening himself would only make it worse.

Joseph stood, unmoving, for a long time, still wanting to make his way into Sally's room. Would it be any safer in there, he wondered? His heart was still thumping and he knew the thought of walking back to the car before morning scared him more than staying in the cabin. The black moving shapes of trees at night had always worried him. He was cold now, too, the sweat wet clothes sticking uncomfortably to his back.

Eventually he collected himself enough to move his feet but he couldn't get his chest to expand enough to breathe freely. He crept slowly down the corridor towards Sally's room, testing the strength of the boards each time before putting down his full weight. He pushed the door open fully and as he moved into the room the chill light of dawn was just visible through the broken window and he could see the shape of the room quite clearly. Suddenly he was flooded by memories, a picture of Sally's face came to mind more vivid than any photo he kept at home, her animated features looming large in front of his vision, bobbing a kiss onto his childish forehead. He saw the gold crucifix shimmering round her neck and remembered her most special of treats, when she allowed him to look through the pendants from her jewelry box. She seemed to be in the room with him.

He breathed deeply, feeling the tension flood out of him. He would be okay now. He now had an image of Sally strong enough to blot out nightmares. He walked round the room, touching the walls and the items of furniture still left, shaking the last drop of light from the flashlight to help him recall the room and his mother. The big items were still here after all these years then, he thought. Sally had taken only what could be heaved onto a train by a lone mother and her child, two cases at most or possibly a trunk if someone could be found with the goodwill to drive her to the train, and the stigma of her old profession so strong her furniture was neither bought or looted by the local people.

There must be something in the room, he thought, something he could take back with him to keep the thought of Sally alive during his long troubled nights. He searched among the decay for a while but most things he touched came apart in his hands. Her beautiful shawl was pinned to the wall but it fell almost to dust as he tried to take it down. How could she have left it behind? She must have been intensely practical, to reduce their lives to the essential ingredients which could be carried to a new life and a new start. She had sacrificed much of the material goods she treasured to give her son a chance of life without the stigma that surrounded her. Joseph wiped the mildewed dust from his hands and searched on, methodically, knowing he would find something. It was growing lighter too, making the task easier.

When he found the pile of linen sheets in the cupboard he knew he would be okay. They were clammy and heavy with damp but they summed up a wonderful picture of being tucked into bed, sandwiched tight between Sally's starched crisp white sheets that smelled of soap and sun dried fresh breezes. He pulled one of the sheets from the stack and kissed it, just for good measure. Then he determined to write the last part of his fear, casting it into words he could look at in the light of day, enclosing it safely so it couldn't hurt him in the dark of his dreams. He walked gingerly back down the rotting passage to the kitchen and found there was now enough light to write by if he pulled the green rug nearer the window. It was cold but he wrapped himself in the sheet and blew some life into his frozen fingers. He would write this important part, he told himself, and then he could go back for a hot bath and breakfast.

He started to write, letting the pen and the words take back the fear that had dominated his life. He felt he could now face the Witchunter General.

The worst day for Poppy was just before her friend Sarah Fletcher died. First the two guards came again as they did once or twice a day, usually as often as there was any food to bring. Fred was the younger one and he called the old guard Pug. This time they took Poppy back down to the dark room again, the one in the cellar, and she knew the man would be there waiting for her, the one who had sat behind her and forced the linen strips into her mouth, his arm gripping iron tight round her shoulders so she couldn't move.

It was so dark she could barely see him in the shadows but this time she was watching for him. The two guards turned her around quickly but she thought she saw the other man briefly, a black mask covering his face and neck.

The younger guard Fred seemed even more uncomfortable than before. He looked away from her and pretended to rearrange the metal implements on the table while Pug removed Poppy's clothing. Poppy focused on the spots of blood dripping from a small scratch where his knife caught her at the chest, not wanting to know what lay in wait for her body that was now totally bare. She wasn't sure if she had ever stood naked before in her life. Whenever she had washed and dressed in the hut with Heliotrope she had slid between her shift and a long piece of cotton sheeting.

She tried to look away but her eyes were drawn back to the dirty face of the guard in front of her. Pug swung her breasts until they bounced against each other and she could see the saliva pooling in his lower lip that hung open as he chuckled. Two of his teeth were missing on one side and the dribble slipped through and hung precariously. He was running his hands over Poppy when the man in the shadows coughed to draw attention to himself. When he spoke, Poppy recognized the voice of the Witchunter General.

'Later,' he told Pug.

Fred snapped to attention but kept his eyes on the floor. Pug moved more slowly but set to work. He attached some chains to Poppy's leg irons then walked away to a wooden wheel that stood some feet away. As Pug slowly turned the wheel so the snake of iron chain on the floor began to move and the slack was taken up. It wasn't until Poppy felt the tug on her ankles that she realized what was intended. As the chain on the ground grew shorter so her feet were in danger of being pulled to the rafters.

The worst of it was the few moments before she was hauled off the ground, watching the snake of chain and knowing what would happen, feeling the sudden tug on her legs and knowing she must do all she could to go with it, to lower her body weight to the floor before her legs were pulled up or else her head would smash on the flagstones. And it wasn't too awful at the start; just her hair in her eyes then knowing her naked skin was open to the men looking at her.

It took a few minutes for the leg manacles to bite into her ankles and the shift in her body weight to register as a great pain in her chest and her breathing. She felt sick too, but the she knew it was mostly fear that turned her stomach. It was difficult to focus as she swung round, Pug laughing to himself and slapping her on the buttocks to make her spin, but Poppy noticed the smell of hot coals and searched round for the brazier she found eventually. The Witchunter, in his leather mask, was showing a nervous Fred how to blow up the coals with a bellows and how to heat branding irons in the fire.

She watched them both as her body swung gently, unable to take her eyes from the two of them no matter how hard she tried to focus on other things. She spent several minutes attempting to form Heliotrope's face in her mind but it was an impossibility, it belonged to a world she had left far behind. She dredged her mind for words that held pictures, anything to blot out the sight of the fire that would cook her flesh, and the only thing that came to her aid was Mistress Spider wrapped in silk to keep away Old Johnny the ague. It seemed a very odd thing but Poppy clung to it all the same, at last able to close her eyes and picture a spider in as much detail as she could remember.

It was then a voice interrupted her thoughts, snapping her back to the brazier and the hot coals. She opened her eyes and found him close to her, his breath warm and close to her breasts that hung oddly upside down.

'You will condemn others,' he whispered, 'I guarantee it.'

It was him, she was certain now, the eyes peering out from the leather hood and piercing into her like pokers. It was the Witchunter General, the man so pious in the cell with her, asking her to repent, proffering his god of salvation, yet now running his hands over her flesh and shaking from the excitement of it.

Joseph kept writing until his notebook was full but he knew he couldn't stop until it was all purged from him. He was finally facing his worst fears, dredging his mind for those dreadful fairy stories put there long ago and locked so far out of reach he had been unable to draw them out. He used the back and front covers of the notebook and then searched through the fishing bag for anything else he could write on. He wanted the words captured and pinned firmly to a place he could see them when he needed to, like tormenting moths lured and finally mounted harmless behind glass. There was a brown paper carrier that he could use. He kept the handwriting small so the paper would last.

It was later, much later, that the young guard Fred explained to the burned and bloodied Poppy how he would leave the door unbarred after his duties that night and that she might avail herself of a walk at any time before sunrise the next morning when he would be forced to check the bolts again. The saddest part for Poppy was not that she could barely walk but that she was leaving behind Sarah who was dead already.

Joseph didn't stop writing until his story had folded a full circle back to the happier times for Poppy, the moments she had with Tom that he had written that evening while he was fishing. He wondered if Hester remembered the good times too. He saw them as fully formed pictures in his head, knowing them as surely as his favorite movie, even though they were just words whispered to him so long ago. He had written everything he knew now, he felt sure, and he just hoped he had been true to Hester's telling of it.

The sun was up and Joseph could tell the day was warming up

outside, for all that his own skin felt chilled from a night spent awake and uncomfortable. He folded the brown paper carrier as carefully as he could with stiff, cold, fingers and placed it with the full notebook. Then he eased his sore joints and tried to stand up. His body was tired beyond belief but he wasn't ready for sleep. He might even type up these chapters when he was fed and bathed.

Chapter 17

Joseph didn't go back to the faucet that day. He typed through into the afternoon, rushing against a self-imposed deadline to catch the store that would run off a copy of the draft. The book wasn't finished but the main elements were in place, and the story drew to a close. Joseph knew how it ended. The stories had all been there, locked in his head.

And Joseph knew he would be heading for home the following day. It seemed he had everything he came for. He would go back to New York and work up a final draft. Or maybe not. Perhaps the whole point had been for him to understand.

He took the disk into town and got his printout, and selected a pretty tin full of chocolates for Old Loula and asked for it to be gift-wrapped. Then he drove back to the hotel to pack his case. He wouldn't be sad to see the back of this place and return home. There was a moment when he considered staying until the weekend, to get in a little fishing, but he was anxious to get away. He put the fishing gear in the trunk of his car and spent the evening watching bad films on the television in his room before taking an early night.

The next morning he was so tired he wasn't sure it was safe to start the drive back home but he paid his bill and carried his luggage to the car. He drove to the clearing and parked as he had most mornings, finding it odd to know he would soon be back in such a different world, in the city. He was just about getting the hang of the slow pace in these parts.

He went to the faucet, to thank Old Loula and to hold Hester's hand one last time. She was his only living relative now. Most of his own skeletons had been aired and were now safely back in the cupboard. He understood about the eyes and for that he would find a way to forgive this strange middle-aged remote woman who smothered the life away from the baby that could have been his cousin. A boy too. That would have been welcome.

Old Loula was nowhere to be seen but Hester was just shuffling out to the water faucet, to read from the small book in her pocket. He watched her gazing at the sky for a while, knowing she would soon take her place and begin to read.

'I am free to call in the libary any day I please,' she said, the words

175

mumbled and spoken to the faucet but Joseph believed they were meant for his benefit. He didn't know if he had heard her speak before.

Hester turned away so he could not see her face and she let the water run into her plastic pail. Slowly she looked down at herself and he followed the gaze to her old shoes, dusty and gray except where the water splashed.

'There is no fetching water and keeping your shoes dry,' she said.

Today was Wednesday, he thought, and she would be nearing the end of her second book and must be careful not to read too quickly. She said nothing more but sat down on the fishing stool she had come to adopt as her own and opened the page she had marked by a leaf.

Now his own book was finally shaped he wondered if he would ever start the business of persuading a publisher to print it. He looked at Hester and she allowed her eyes to meet his. It was as if she was reading his thoughts.

Joseph thought he had come to understand Hester better over the past days. She lived in two worlds and he knew which one she preferred. If she shut out the screeching of that young cockerel and the sight of him strutting around amongst the chickens by the faucet then she could get one part of herself to fade while she turned up the volume on the other life. She liked it better at Mistley Thorn, kicking her feet free in the cool grass outside the Thorn Inn, watching the sailors watching her legs. Why would she want to come back to the hurt that lay in wait for her at the faucet?

It was some time before Old Loula arrived. Joseph had brought her the present and was waiting to thank her; otherwise he could have gone early, straight from the hotel. She walked slowly up to him, guessing he would leave that morning, so when she first tried to detain him with more stories he was ready to make his excuses. His suitcase was packed and in the trunk and it was a long drive. But Old Loula placed a hand on his arm and persuaded him to stay for just a few minutes more.

His sat, more out of politeness than a need to hear more. The old woman had given him the gift he needed. She had shown there was another side to Solomon. Maybe it could never balance the uglier tales, but Joseph needed to know his grandfather had started life as a caring man. He had also come to know Old Loula was the woman who should have been his grandmother and that meant a lot to a man with no family. He couldn't tell if Old Loula herself had worked it out but he thought perhaps she had. He decided to leave it at that and thanked her formally, offering the small present he had brought with him. Old Loula didn't seem to notice but looked over to one small cloud that was drifting slowly, high up in the sky, alone.

It was then Hester looked up and he knew he wanted to give her the patched and rewritten manuscript that was in the car. He could always print himself another copy back home.

Joseph walked to the car and came back with the papers, hoping Hester would understand why he had to write it down. She allowed him to place the pages in her hands.

It was when he turned to shake hands finally with Old Loula that he got a shock. Old Loula had shrunk down into herself and was mumbling, either to him or to herself, he couldn't be sure.

'I know what Hester sees when she comes to the seat now and looks at me,' Old Loula said, her voice whining like a child's. 'Someone small, dry and old on the bench, and as I run my hands over my speckle gray hair I feel it short and spiky, same as my temper Sissie Jane would say. All she sees is a old woman resting her gnarled feet on a rusty pail, and that old pail bald of its enamel now. I see Hester look up at us three women sometimes and I feel I know what she sees; the whiteness of Sissie Jane's hair, the scalp showing through at the crown with the hair now so sparse. And Libby gazing down at her bunions.'

Two elderly ladies were walking slowly into the clearing, one was fat and had trouble walking, the taller woman was hunched over a stick and the few hairs she had left were as white as cotton tufts. He was about to walk over and introduce himself, feeling it must surely be Sissie Jane and Libby at last, but Old Loula's voice became louder and she gripped his arm to keep him at her side.

'I know what they says,' continued Old Loula. 'Senile and no longer knowing what is happening, that is what they say about me. I know,' she went on. 'Maybe it is true. It don't bother me none if folks think that of me. I is just a little hard of hearing and perhaps it is easier for me to stick to watching. Hester and me have that it common. Just four old women at the spigot.'

177

Joseph couldn't make it out. He was beginning to doubt his own memory of the past week and the engrossing stories he had heard.

'There is a faucet in every house now anyways,' said Old Loula. She pulled Joseph closer to her. 'I see you watching the whiteness of Sissie Jane's hair,' she said, not loosening her grip on his arm. 'So fine and pure against her wrinkled black old skin, and the scalp showing through. Sissie the wisewoman, our medic, bringing folks into the world, keeping them alive then helping them back up to God when he calls. Six foot tall and more she has been, in the days before she started to hunch over and shrink down on her stick. Practical, caring and still full of the love of Jesus.'

The two women arrived at the faucet and Hester shuffled her stool further from the bench to make room for them. She looked down at her book as before and the two old women eased their bodies onto the seat. Sissie Jane and Libby did not acknowledge Joseph but carried on talking to each other.

'He refreshes and restores our life,' said Sissie Jane, trying to end a discussion that seemed to have been going on for some time. Her voice was clear but tinged with the quake of an old woman. 'Psalm 23:2,' she said.

The short round one looked over the rolls of her own flesh, down at her feet. 'If Jesus had my bunions he would see things different, I can't help feeling,' she lisped through her toothless gums.

'Just goes to prove what good footwear the Lord supplies to the righteous,' countered Sissie Jane.

Finally there was a break in the talking and Joseph felt able to introduce himself, but Old Loula would not let go of him. She pulled him nearer so she could speak right into his ear.

'Before, it was Libby was the nearest we had to a intellectual,' she whispered. 'She could write her own name and had heard of things way beyond the place we live. It was Libby as taught Hester to read, although her belief that the tail of a Y came on the left and curved to the right rather than the other way around made things difficult for Hester at the start. Libby has no teeth at all these days, making her speech as crazy as her spelling has always been. She daydreams a lot too, I know that for a fact, although many see it as plain vacancy, but she is spending these later years reflecting on her youth. It is a might better than reflecting on the current state of her bunions is how she tells of it.'

Joseph had tried pulling away but the old woman's fingers had only tightened more, so he went for a different approach. He reached down to where she sat on the bench and gave her shoulders a comforting squeeze, wondering how many decades must have gone by since she had been touched by anyone. He felt her relax at last so he kissed her gently on the cheek and this time she let her fingers loosen and drop. With great care he patted the top of her old head and then turned to walk towards the car, waving goodbye to the two newcomers. He could still hear Old Loula talking to herself.

'She is a nice girl that Jenny, the librarian, a little blond thing of only sixteen or so when she started, but it took her the most part of a year before she was able to find the right kind of books that Hester likes to read. It was trial and error to begin but now their little system works a treat. But Jenny doesn't work in the library these days, I am confused there, Jenny can't work, what with her needing to mind the grandchildren for her daughter-in-law who has a job in a store, but she does call in of a Thursday morning each other week to browse the shelves and find just the right books for Hester to check through.

Clem will run Hester into town in his pick-up on each alternate Thursday and she will check out two books. It always takes her a week each to read them.'

Chapter 18

POPPY'S STORY - THE FINAL CHAPTER

The Good Lord only knows what goes on in her head these days, said Old Loula, for she says little to the likes of me and I don't know another fool as would set on a bench or rocker for hours and just listen to her ramblings.

The thoughts that Hester really played through her mind were split half and half, and neither bore much resemblance to what Old Loula imagined. People were funny about Hester now so she kept them out. These days she spent a lot of time in Manningtree and Mistley Thorn. She liked it better there with the cool swirling sea mist and her Yarb Mother, Heliotrope. Sometimes it was too hot by the faucet.

If Hester's other life was a set of video tapes for her to watch as she chose, then the ones worn thin were the best and the worst of it, her short time with Tom and those long weeks with the Witchunter General. These had not lost their color with continued use but had gained vibrancy with each repeat until they were more real now than Hester's life at the faucet. Tom, her lover at last, was in better focus than Old Loula, and the mornings when this show ran, Hester would gaze unseeing at the pages of the book in front of her and a brightness burned in her eyes that some took for madness. It was mostly at night the other tape played again and again. But the sound was too good, the contrast too sharp and even the pain came through, and there was no control to turn it back down.

But Hester liked the Tom show best of all.

The sea mists cleared away and the sun streamed in shafts through all the loose loft boards to warm her body as Tom slowly took off her clothes. She smiled as she watched his face change in wonder with each new part of her exposed. He saw past the fresh scars, as she knew he would, and wondered at the body underneath. He slipped her cotton shift over her shoulders and down her arms then stared at her breasts for a full minute before reaching up to touch her bare skin. They were sitting on the loose hay, she kneeling and him half laying beside her. At last he stretched out a hand and cupped her flesh, pulling her gently toward him as he leant into her and rested his cheek against her. She was happy then. Happy to see the joy on his face and feel the warm kind breath of him brushing her pale skin. She laughed and bent her head to kiss him.

'Take me to the barn Tom,' she had told him that morning, knowing there was so little time left before the Witchunter General would find her again. 'Take me to the barn and do what men do.'

He had protested, but finally she had got him to understand the panic in her. The fear she might die without knowing his love. Now Tom looked up at her, his great shock of straw colored hair falling into his eyes.

'Will you let me marry you,' he asked, 'because I fear to spoil you if you say no.'

How could she tell him there was no time? That she now doubted she could live that long? That she must take her own life with dignity or allow others to rob it from her in the name of their god. That she could never go back to that bleak cell. Heliotrope was speaking with the Witan council that morning saying it was only the beginning, that all along Poppy had been right, the Witchunter was coming for them all.

Poppy saw forward to the water and maybe she wasn't ready for that yet. She kept her thoughts focused on Tom's breath, warm on her body, his soft hot lips touching so very slowly over her breasts, him nuzzling the smell of her freshly washed skin. She laughed to realize how much she wanted him to press against her, how she wanted him to see every part of her body, how happy she would be to have him touch and love her small arm and her thin leg.

'Tom,' she whispered.

'Yes,' he asked, leaving her breasts reluctantly and sitting up to face her.

'I am just taking pleasure in saying your name,' she said, laughing again.

His serious face broke into a smile and he rose nimbly to his feet, pulling her gently after him. She struggled out of the sleeves of her shift to bare the whole of her chest and Tom reached to find the strings of her skirt. Poppy took his hands and placed them on his own breeches.

'It is your turn now,' she said.

He raised an eyebrow and put his head on one side, looking at her.

'Yes,' she said.

He stripped off quickly then, laughing and happy as he threw his clothing in the air, tossing shirt, undershirt and breeches down from the loft to the floor of the barn. He danced naked for her, his parts so hard and strong and proudly dancing their own jig for her. She knew then that she trusted Tom to love her well.

He was more serious now and pulling at her skirt strings, but he had them knotted up with the ties from her petticoats and she had to help him. Finally she stood naked too and they stopped to wonder at each other. He took her small hand and kissed it, then he touched the poppy red birthmark on her thigh and skirted lightly over the raw burns branded into her flesh. Then he kissed the yellowed bruises with warm soft lips. Poppy stood straight and proud on her strong leg, feeling more beautiful than she had ever dreamed. When he had drunk her in, he stepped close to her and their skin touched, chest to chest, thigh to thigh, her head into his shoulder. He swallowed her up in his embrace and she slipped her hands in under his arms and found the tight muscles of his behind. His flesh was solid, quite unlike her own, and her fingers rested comfortably on his skin. At the same time he was kneading and stroking the curve of her buttocks and thighs, discovering flesh that gave softly to the touch.

She felt him hard and warm on her bare skin, pressing against her ribs, but this time she was not afraid.

It was Tom's love that gave her the strength to join the women the next morning.

We must hold hands, Heliotrope told them; hold hands as we walk together into the water. United. No Hopkins to divide us. The water will cool us, she said. Cool the fire of accusations.

Hopkins, the Witchunter General, was coming to find them all with his list of names. The Witan council had called a meeting and Meg Southly, her highland voice ringing out harsh against the soft tones of the others, said it was only Poppy the Witchunter was really after, using the poppy red mark Nathaniel claimed was burned there by the devil's claw when the devil himself took her maidenhead. But it was not just Poppy's name that sat on the list, said others. Hopkins was traveling all of Norfolk and Essex it was said, leaving no village or hamlet unchecked for witches. The Witchunter General would strip them all, checking for himself, looking for marks and expecting maidenheads intact on all unmarried women and claiming the devil had taken any that were missing, because that was the law. Poppy said to Heliotrope and the others that she would flee from Manningtree and Mistley Thorn before he caught her again but they said it was no use, that he had them all marked down for a pricking and a hanging, that he would strip them and paw at their bodies looking for the devil's mark before they were thrown into gaol. Most would be tortured to confess their joining in wedlock with the devil and only the lucky ones would be allowed to die easily.

Heliotrope said they should not wait for trouble to come to them but should ask their friend the water to help before it was too late. Water had always been their friend, she reminded them, and the council decided they should remain together, and if that meant united together as souls while their bodies died, then so be it. Only Meg stole away.

Now Heliotrope took Poppy's hand, the small one, the left hand, and held it gently. With great relief Poppy found she was finally able to step outside herself again and could see it two ways, seeing from her eyes along her arm, feeling the warmth of Heliotrope against her own skin, and then another way, outside herself, looking as Heliotrope took the small crippled hand of Poppy. This time she saw it from higher, from outside. Heliotrope had always looked after her, Poppy her daughter in all ways other than birth. It was a promise she'd made nearly seventeen years before, drawing the child from her dead mother's body. The water was the only way she could protect her now. The only way. To keep her from being hung as a witch. This way she could die amongst friends. Poppy knew this, yet still she was afraid.

Heliotrope looked round at the faces, those waiting her word to walk into the water. She was a portly woman, great ruddy cheeks and her shining eyes bulging that way. Poppy knew others found her fierce and considered her quite an awesome figure, her energy and her rage being far too similar for many to see the difference. She could only guess they missed the twinkle in her eye that gave the game away.

Poppy looked around now. There was peace in every face. Resolute peace. All faces except her own.

'Isis, Istase, Diana,' Heliotrope mouthed her incantation and they followed.

And Poppy looked around again, knowing some were sacrificing more than others for many might be spared or could flee to safety, yet still they did it, finding strength in a common defiance. All preferring to die free. None to hold back in the hope they might be the one to escape the Witchunter General. Most would be accused, perhaps, but some could be tried and freed. Not herself though, thought Poppy, not with one side of her body withered. She looked up at Heliotrope's rugged body and watched the moving lips of the other women, their hair catching wet in the salt wind and whipping their faces. Poppy knew she, like they, was whole inside. But she knew too that Hopkins and his church folk would judge only what they saw.

'You take my hand Poppy,' said Heliotrope as she brought the poor shriveled hand to her own lips and kissed it. 'Never let go,' she told her. 'I will always be here.'

Then she raised her voice and spoke out for the others to hear.

'Women are dying to be free. The earth is a wicce and the men still burn her. Isis, Istase, Diana ... take hands and let the water feed and grow fat on our power, the power so feared by those men who are bonded by the man on the cross.'

The others took up the chant. 'Women are dying to be free. The earth is a wicce and the men still burn her. To us the earth is a healer.'

Poppy mouthed the words and watched the lips move on the faces of the other women before her, but the sounds no longer reached her. She was to have been seventeen that year. She still wanted to be seventeen, to see her birthday. To see her Tom again. To feel him even one more time. She didn't want to die. Not yet. There were so many things she wanted to do, and yet the others were going so willingly, not blaming her for dragging them to these last moments, no one accusing her of bringing the Witchunter or Nathaniel's anger to their community, all of them walking through the marshes of Tendring Hundred. She watched herself dragging behind a little; the wind catching in her loose hair, trying to make out it was the lame foot that slowed her.

Then the mud wet chilled her feet and she was happy to return to her body again. Heliotrope squeezed her strong red paw and flooded strength into her hand. Poppy took the hand of the woman on her right and passed the squeeze along. It was something they did in their worship, passing their love from one to another. Heliotrope taught them always to be selfless with their love. Hate was too powerful a force to unleash, Heliotrope said. They must never hate. Hopkins hated and he brought his devil alongside him, thought Poppy, but then she remembered what Heliotrope had taught her, that the devil was an invention of the Christians. They made their one god, their god of love they called him, made him so good there was no room for any blemish. Life must have blemishes, and so they made a devil to be responsible for all the things their perfect god could not be associated with. But Poppy, Heliotrope and the women had many gods, all a balance of good and bad combined, with whims, and tempers, and generosity. They had no need to invent a devil.

The mud squelched between their toes now and the sea mist hid the sight of Poppy's feet from her, hid the sight of her toes, and the stones she must stumble on, and the limbs of her friends as they floated together through the mist. She was their equal now. Her legs their equal. Her two legs equal to each other at last. No stick leg to be seen. They floated together in mist. Soon it would all be water.

They didn't start to sing until they felt the water round their thighs. Then Heliotrope broke off to whisper to Poppy, to tell her there would be other times, other lives. That this one had run

185

out. Come now, with pride, she told her. Don't let them drag you screaming to a wicce's hanging. Choose to go. It is your choice.

The trouble was, Poppy wasn't sure this was her choice.

'Are you sure I will come back?' she asked, although parts of her remembered and doubted it less than her physical self.

'I promise you,' said Heliotrope.

THE END

Printed in the United Kingdom
by Lightning Source UK Ltd.
131430UK00001B/25/P